THE RUPERT
ANNUAL

EXPRESS NEWSPAPERS

First published in Great Britain 2022 by Farshore
An imprint of HarperCollins*Publishers*
1 London Bridge Street, London SE1 9GF
www.farshore.co.uk

HarperCollins*Publishers*
1st Floor, Watermarque Building, Ringsend Road
Dublin 4, Ireland

RUPERT BEAR © & TM Express Newspapers & DreamWorks Distribution Limited. All rights reserved.

ISBN 978 0 0085 0768 8
Printed in Romania
001

MIX
Paper from
responsible sources
FSC™ C007454

No. 87

RUPERT and POLL

RUPERT STOPS TO LOOK

*"My pals are staring at the tree!
I wonder what it is they see."*

*The chums say, "We can't see from here,
But Rastus noticed something queer!"*

Rupert is coming home from the shops when he sees his pals near a tree. "Hallo," he says, "I wonder why they are staring up into the branches. I must go and see." As he turns to cross the grass a little cat scampers up to him. "You're a pretty puss," says Rupert. "Where have you come from and what's your name?" The cat purrs and rubs against Rupert's legs, and the little bear stops for a moment to stroke the friendly creature. Then he hears his chums talking among themselves and he hurries on to join them. The little cat runs after him, and then leaps up the tree, soon disappearing among the leaves. "I wonder what he's after," says Rupert, "and what are you all gazing at?" "Rastus *thinks* he saw something brightly coloured up there," says Edward, "but he's not sure about it."

6

PARROT

On the next eight pages are small pictures of the Guides signalling a message to you with semaphore flags. Each signal stands for an alphabet letter. If you are unable to read the code message, turn to page 15 for the answer.

RUPERT CALLS EDWARD BACK

As Edward Trunk goes on his way
The little bear calls out, "Please stay!"

"There's something up there all the time,"
Says Rupert as he starts to climb.

"Ah, well," adds Edward, "we must get on with our errands now. Perhaps Rastus was dreaming!" "It wasn't a dream – I was wide awake," insists Rastus. "I certainly did see something and it seemed to be hopping from branch to branch." "It might have been a bit of coloured paper blown about by the wind," laughs Edward. "Come along. We can't stay here all day." They all turn away but Rupert still peers into the branches of the tree. Suddenly he sees a flash of colour high in the tree-top. "Hey, Edward!" he cries, "I can see it too! Do come here!" Edward runs back, and they both gaze excitedly. "I think I could get up this tree if I could climb on your back," says Rupert. So, while Edward stands very steady, Rupert balances carefully on his pal's shoulders and manages to reach a branch.

RUPERT COAXES THE PARROT

Gasps Rupert, "Fancy seeing that!
A parrot, sitting near a cat!"

"Look, here's a biscuit," Rupert cries,
And to his hand the parrot flies.

"I wish that I could stop and play,"
Says Edward, "But I mustn't stay."

And at the gate stands Mrs Bear,
Who says, "Now what have you got there?"

Up and up goes Rupert and suddenly, straight in front of him, he sees the little cat sitting on a branch, close to a brightly-coloured parrot. "So it was a parrot we saw," he cries, "and he's certainly good friends with the cat! This is a queer business!" He quickly climbs down and tells Edward all about it. "I'm going to try and get him down," he says, taking a biscuit from his bag, and holding it out. Sure enough, the parrot flies down for it and perches on Rupert's arm quite comfortable, while the little cat clambers down the tree to his friend. "Oh dear! It's time for me to go," says Edward, and sets off alone, while Rupert takes the parrot back to his house, with the cat following. Mrs Bear meets them at the gate, and soon gives him some more biscuits for the bird. "Now I must find who owns these two," says Rupert.

RUPERT LISTENS WITH PAULINE

"Perhaps he'll talk – I haven't tried,"
Says Rupert to Pauline the Guide.

They listen while Poll clicks away,
And wonder what he wants to say.

"He doesn't talk – he clicks in Morse!
That's what the noises mean, of course!"

"Let's ask my friends. Maybe they'll know,"
The Girl Guide says, so off they go.

As Rupert turns away he meets Pauline the Guide. She is very eager to hear the parrot talk. "Let's give him a bit of biscuit," she adds. "Perhaps he'll say, 'thank you'." But the parrot eats his biscuit without a word, then flies to the branch of a nearby tree and begins to make queer clicking noises. "How funny he is," laughs Pauline and then stops suddenly. "Listen!" she cries excitedly, "is it–?

Yes, it *is*!" "Is *what*?" asks Rupert. "What are you excited about?" "Why, you listen to the way he clicks his tongue!" cries Pauline. "It is just like a message in Morse code." Rupert is very surprised. "Then what is he saying?" he gasps. "Well, I can't quite make it out! I'm not very good at Morse," says Pauline, "but the other Guides may know. Come on! I know where to find them."

RUPERT HEARS THE MESSAGE

"Well, that's a thing I'd like to hear!"
Laughs Beryl, "What a strange idea!"

"Keep still," says Rupert, "then you'll see
The parrot will fly down to me!"

They all sit quietly on the ground,
And listen to the clicking sound.

"It's really Morse code!" Beryl cries,
And reads the words in great surprise.

Before long Pauline is telling her story to Beryl and Janet. "What a crazy idea!" laughs Beryl, the eldest of the three, who ever heard of a Morse parrot?" Let's hear him." So Rupert holds out some more biscuit to the parrot, who has perched on a nearby tree. The Guides keep quite still, and in a moment the parrot is flying down towards them. "You certainly love biscuit, old boy," chuckles Rupert, as the bird settles on his arm and nibbles the piece. Directly he has eaten the biscuit and the parrot begins clicking away, and Beryl jots down everything the bird says. Soon she has written a number of dots and dashes, and then she jumps up, looking very astonished. "You're right!" she cries, "These clickings make real words! Listen!" and she reads out, "VIGO, ADEN, GOA, S.O.S., RIO!"

RUPERT REACHES THE SHACK

"Maybe a sailor owns this pet,"
Says Janet. "We may solve it yet!"

Up Rupert jumps, and off he strides,
"Sam's sure to know," he tells the Guides.

"Sam isn't home to-day, I fear,
It looks as though there's no one here."

Nearby a window's open wide,
The pets now disappear inside.

"Well, this *is* a queer business!" cries Rupert. "Let's see what we can make of it!" They murmur the strange words aloud, and then Janet suddenly says, "Those words are nearly all the names of sea ports! This parrot may belong to a sailor!" "Right!" says Rupert, jumping to his feet. "Then we'll ask Sailor Sam! He's the only seaman round here." He leads the way to Sailor Sam's shack. The little cat runs along beside him, and the parrot flies overhead. But when Rupert reaches the shack, no one answers his knock. Suddenly he hears a scratching sound, and, looking round, he sees the cat scrambling up to an open window, through which the parrot is flying. "Well, they seem at home here," he cries, "they must belong to Sailor Sam." "Janet's idea was certainly right!" exclaims Beryl.

Rupert and Poll Parrot

RUPERT FINDS SAM IN BED

"I'm sure that someone must be there.
Let's knock again," says Rupert Bear.

"Please lift me to the window sill!
I'm going in – perhaps Sam's ill!"

There, in a bunk built in the wall,
Lies Sam, not looking well at all.

"Poor Sam is really very bad!"
Sighs Rupert, looking rather sad.

"Where is Sam?" murmurs Rupert as he knocks again. He and the Guides wait awhile, listening carefully. "Come in!" says a weak voice from inside the shack, but when Rupert tries the door, it is locked. "This is rather worrying!" he frowns. "If only I could climb through that window!" "That's easy!" says Janet, and, lifting him up, she helps him scramble over the window sill. Inside the shack,

Rupert finds Sailor Sam lying in a bunk built into the wall. "You *do* look ill!" he cries and explains why he has come. Sam gives a weak chuckle. "Been practising my Morse," he whispers, "couldn't manage bigger words – such a long time since I used it – parrot must have mimicked me! Oh dear! I do feel bad! It's my old complaints again!" Rupert feeling very worried, opens the door and tells the Guides.

RUPERT HUNTS FOR DR LION

"I'm certain that it would be wise
To fetch the doctor," Beryl cries.

"We'll find the doctor soon," they say,
"If each one goes a different way."

Cries Rupert thankfully, "Hurrah!
I'm sure that's Doctor Lion's car!"

"Our sailor friend is ill," says he,
"So, Doctor, will you come with me?"

"There's only one thing to do," says Beryl as Rupert finishes his story, "we must go and fetch Dr Lion at once! But he will be on his rounds now, so there is no knowing what part of the village he may have reached. We had better go in different directions, then one of us will be more likely to meet him." Quickly she gives her order, and Rupert and the others run off. The little bear dashes down the hill and into the village at top speed. Suddenly, turning a corner, he sees a car ahead of him. "I do believe that's Dr Lion's car!" he gasps. "I must hurry, or he will be off to another patient!" He gallops along the road for all he is worth and as he draws closer, he sees Dr Lion coming out of the house. "Thank goodness I have found you," cries Rupert, and gasps out his story of Sailor Sam's plight.

RUPERT RIDES WITH THE DOCTOR

Off drives the doctor, very fast,
And Pauline sees the car rush past.

The doctor hurries up the track
That leads him to the sailor's shack.

"I'll feed the parrot and the cat,
I'm very glad I thought of that!"

"He can't be moved – he must lie still,"
The doctor says, "he's very ill!"

Dr Lion listens carefully. "Hum! I must see him at once," he says. "Jump in Rupert!" As they drive off quickly, Rupert and Pauline catch a glimpse of each other, and the Guide runs to tell her chums that the doctor has been found. Dr Lion drives as far as he can, and then Rupert leads the way to Sailor Sam's shack. As they get near the house the little cat runs to meet Rupert, looking very pleased to see him again. Rupert takes Doctor Lion straight to Sailor Sam's bunk, and while the doctor examines him Rupert hunts for some food and feeds both the parrot and the cat. When Dr Lion has finished, he turns to Rupert. "It's lucky you fetched for me, for Sam is very ill," he says. Rupert explains the whole story. "It was all because Poll Parrot had learnt to click his tongue in Morse!" he chuckles.

"I hope that we aren't very late,"
Says Beryl, running to the gate.

"The nurse will find us jobs to do.
And we can run the errands, too!"

Sighs Rupert, "How relieved I am
That, thanks to you, we've found poor Sam!"

So each of Rupert's pals decides
To do his best to help the Guides.

The Guides have arrived, and Rupert runs on ahead of Dr Lion to tell them the news. "I shall send for a trained nurse," says the doctor, "for, even if Sam could be moved, the hospital is full." "Oh, do let us help!" cries Beryl eagerly, "We can run errands to the village and we can help the nurse, too." The idea pleases Dr Lion, and with a kindly nod he returns to his car and drives off. "That's fine!" says Beryl, "we shall all be able to do our good deeds for many days!" "You have done one already," smiles Rupert, "for you recognised Poll Parrot's Morse, and that led us to Sailor Sam." Then he runs to tell his pals all about it. "There's a grand job for us to do," he says. "While the Guides help the nurse, we can take care of Sam's pets and tend his garden until he is well enough to get up!" The End.

Redirected Post

No wonder the postmen couldn't deliver these letters!
Can you work out who they are for?

DINKBO

PIGG PONN

LOOTNITE

ODGYP

TERPUR

RUPERT ®

and
April Showers

RUPERT OFFERS TO HELP

Though Rupert Bear has been away,
His uncle brings him home today.

"I'm back!" calls Rupert. Then he sees,
His mother, searching, on her knees.

She's lost a jigsaw piece – just one –
And now the puzzle can't be done.

"A shame," his mum says, with dismay,
As Rupert heads outside to play.

Rupert Bear has been away, visiting his favourite uncle. They've had a wonderful holiday together, with lots of walks, games and picnics. "Goodbye, Uncle Bruno! And thank you!" Rupert cries, as his uncle drops him back at home. Rupert goes inside, only to find his mummy on her knees, peering under a table. She's very glad to see Rupert, but she seems rather distracted, so the little bear asks what's wrong. "I've lost a piece from my jigsaw," she replies.

Rupert goes over to the coffee table and inspects the puzzle. Although it's a lovely picture of spring, there's one piece missing, right in the middle. "It's such a shame," Mrs Bear says. "It's been missing all week, and I thought I'd try searching once more before giving up." "I'll help you look," Rupert offers, but Mrs Bear suggests he should go out and play while the weather is so nice. "I'll help you find the missing jigsaw piece later," Rupert says as he heads outside.

RUPERT TAKES A STROLL

The grass is green; the air is clear.
Now that Spring is finally here!

He pauses just between the hills,
To sniff the fragrant daffodils.

He greets a bird, who stops to say,
"I must complete my nest today!"

Then suddenly, the rain pours down!
"What's this?" gasps Rupert, with a frown.

It doesn't take long for Rupert to walk to Nutwood Common. His mummy was right: the weather is lovely. It's a warm, spring day, with just a gentle hint of a breeze. Rupert pauses to admire the flowers that have bloomed since he was away. There are budding crocuses and cheerful daffodils. "Today would be the perfect day for a picnic," he muses, "or a game of football. I wonder if my pals are out today?"

"Hello, Rupert!" calls a shrill voice. Rupert looks up and sees a bird carrying a thick twig in her beak. "Hello, how are you?" he replies. "I'm nearly finished with my nest," she tells him proudly. "Just a few more pieces to go. I'll be so relieved when it's complete!" Rupert wishes her good luck, but before he can go much further, it starts to rain! Rupert knows that with spring comes showers, but he's surprised at how heavy the sudden downpour is.

RUPERT SPIES A FACE

He shelters in the trees, and yet . . .
It seems the bear's still getting wet!

Perplexed, the bear peers up and sees
A figure grinning through the leaves.

Before he thinks of what to say,
The tiny figure fades away.

He wonders why she's disappeared.
"Oh well, at least the rain has cleared!"

"If I can just make it to those trees, I can shelter under there until the rain passes," Rupert thinks, and he hurries along. He reaches the large trunk, but something is not right. Although the branches and foliage are thick, Rupert is still getting wet . . . almost as if the raindrops are following him! Perplexed, Rupert looks up. He startles when he sees what looks like a tiny face poking through the leaves, staring back at him with a cheeky smile.

"I say, who are you?" Rupert asks. The figure just grins even more, and then she winks. "What's your name?" Rupert tries again, but she ducks back into the leaves and disappears. Rupert waits for a moment longer, but she doesn't reappear. "Perhaps I imagined it?" he thinks to himself. "In any case, the rain seems to have stopped!" The little bear is still dripping from the earlier downpour. He is just thinking about whether to go back home for dry clothes when he hears a tiny laugh.

Rupert and April Showers
RUPERT SPEAKS TO THE IMPS

He hears a tiny laugh. "Who's there?
I'll check it out," thinks Rupert Bear.

Soon Rupert spies, beside the tree,
A cheeky imp, who squeaks, "Come see."

The bear pursues the imp he's found,
Who leads him deep, down underground.

"Our April Showers makes it rain –
She loves a joke," the imps explain.

"How strange," thinks Rupert, "I'd better see who that is." Rupert follows the sound of laughter. He soon spots who it is. "Why, it's the Imps of Spring!" There are two tiny imps, each dressed in a red tunic with a yellow collar. The imps turn to greet Rupert, and he asks them about the mysterious rain. One of the imps replies, "Why don't you come back with us to dry off, and we'll tell you more . . ."

The Imps of Spring lead Rupert through a tunnel in the bottom of the tree. They scurry along playfully, and Rupert has to rush to keep up, following the tangle of roots deep underground. When they finally reach the imps' den, one of the imps fetches a towel for Rupert to dry off with. Another imp explains: "You must have met April Showers. She's been playing a lot of pranks recently. You see, she flies her rain cloud around, and anyone standing beneath it gets a soaking!"

RUPERT TAKES THE PARCEL

"But what's that box you've tried to hide?"
Asks Rupert Bear, once he's all dried.

"It's just a parcel that I found.
At Nutwood Common, on the ground."

"I'd better take it," says the bear.
"I'll find its owner back up there."

"It's lost its label! If I'm smart,
The post office is where I'll start."t

Rupert finishes drying off, and he spies one imp behind the others, who is looking around nervously. He's holding a small box, when he notices Rupert looking at him, he drops it, flustered. "What's that box you've got?" Rupert asks. The imp sighs, "I might as well tell you. I found this parcel on the ground at Nutwood Common, but the label has torn off. I don't know what it is, and I haven't tried to open it yet."

Rupert inspects the parcel. There's a stamp in the top corner; even though the label with the address is missing, he's sure that it's meant to be some sort of post. "I wonder who ordered it?" Rupert says. "I'd better take it. I can go to the Nutwood Post Office, and we'll work out who it belongs to." The imp agrees to give the parcel to Rupert. So, the little bear waves goodbye, and climbs back up the tunnel.

RUPERT ASKS HIS FRIENDS

*He waves to Pong Ping. "I should ask
If he can help me with my task!"*

*The Pekingese is quite upset.
"That rain cloud came – now I'm all wet!"*

*"I'm going home," he moans, "to dry,
It's not my parcel, so goodbye."*

*"There's Lily Duckling over there.
Perhaps she'll help me," thinks the bear.*

As he continues across Nutwood Common towards town, Rupert sees his chum Pong Ping. He waves at the little Pekingese, thinking, "If the imps found the parcel on Nutwood Common, perhaps Pong Ping dropped it earlier? I might as well go and ask him!" But Pong Ping is in no mood to talk. His fur and lovely black coat are sopping wet, and he's very grumpy. "A rain cloud came out of nowhere and drenched me," he huffs.

Rupert starts to share what the imps explained about April Showers. Then he asks if Pong Ping would like to accompany him to the Nutwood Post Office. Pong Ping shakes his head. "It's not *my* parcel, and I'm too wet to do anything. I'm going back home to dry off." He waves goodbye and squelches home. Rupert continues on and spies a pink bonnet in the distance. "That must be my friend Lily Duckling. I'll go and ask her for help!"

RUPERT AND LILY TAKE SHELTER

As Lily takes in what is said,
A rain cloud pops up overhead!

"Another shower?" Rupert cries.
"Let's shelter here," his friend replies.

A cloud appears between the chums,
And Rupert sighs, as more rain comes.

And with a loud and startled quack,
Poor Lily's off, not looking back!

Lily Duckling listens carefully as Rupert tells her about the mysterious parcel. Lily inspects it, and points to a small bump in the corner. "See this? I wonder if it fell out of Postie's bag while he was on his rounds. Maybe that's when the label fell off, too." "Say, you're probably right," Rupert responds. But just then, the rain starts up again! "Another spring shower? Luckily, I brought my umbrella," Lily says. The friends huddle beneath it as they walk towards town.

Before they've gone too far, something very strange happens. The thick raindrops carry on falling but this time they're coming from *underneath* the umbrella! Rupert recognises the face he saw up in the tree earlier. This must be April Showers, the mischievous imp who likes to play tricks by making it rain on everyone! Lily Duckling can't believe her eyes. With a startled *quack*, she dashes off. "Wait!" Rupert calls after her, but she's already gone.

RUPERT LETS APRIL HELP

He calls to April in the trees,
"Don't rain upon this parcel, please."

"I don't know who dropped it, or why,"
Says Rupert. "But it must stay dry."

"If you'll forgive me," April pleads,
"I'll come and help you with your deeds."

So April zooms off in a blur,
With Rupert chasing after her!

The showers have stopped for now, but Rupert hears a rustling in the trees, and suspects that it's April, waiting for someone else to rain on. "April Showers?" he calls up. "Please don't make it rain again. I'm carrying a very important parcel, and I don't want it to get wet. The Spring Imps found it, and I must work out who it belongs to." At Rupert's words, the little imp comes down from the tree, looking ashamed.

"I'm sorry for nearly ruining your parcel," she says. "But I can help you find its owner; I know I can!" "Thank you," the little bear says. April is thrilled to be part of Rupert's mission, and she promises not to soak the parcel – or Rupert again. "Where do we look first?" she asks. "Well, I was on my way to the Nutwood Post Office . . ." Rupert begins. He's barely finished speaking when April jumps on her rain cloud and speeds off. "Hurry up!" she calls back.

RUPERT SPOTS A LABEL

The little bear runs up the hill,
To speak to Algy Pug and Bill.

"That parcel's not ours," they agree.
And Rupert thinks, "Whose could it be?"

The question plays on Rupert's mind.
(He misses April's tricks behind!)

He sees his friend, the bird, then spies
A label – it's the perfect size!

April races along quickly! She's nearly out of sight when Rupert nears the edge of the common. He stops to catch his breath and spots his chums Bill Badger and Algy Pug. "Hi Rupert, what's the hurry?" Bill laughs. Rupert shows them the parcel and asks if it belongs to either of them. "That's not mine," Algy says. "Or mine," Bill adds. They invite Rupert to play, and the little bear says he'll try and come back later that day.

Rupert waves goodbye to his pals. "I wonder who this parcel could belong to?" he thinks. "It can't have been missing for too long, or else *someone* would be out looking for it!" Rupert is so lost in thought that he doesn't notice what's happening behind him . . . April Showers just can't resist playing a quick trick on Bill and Algy! Soon after, Rupert sees his friend the bird. She's sitting proudly on her finished nest. As Rupert pauses to admire it, he spots something poking out of it.

The bird jumps up; April is stressed . . .
She makes it rain down on the nest!

"Oh dear," cries April. "What to do . . .
The label's wet. You're soaking, too!"

But Rupert has another plan.
"Please, Bingo, help us if you can."

"The ink has run, but never fear –
I'll solve it by these letters here!"

"Look!" Rupert exclaims. "This bit of paper in the nest is just the right size for the parcel's label!" The bird's nest is made up of twigs and scraps she found on Nutwood Common. "I was in too much of a hurry to look at it closely, but let's look now!" the bird says. She flutters upward so quickly that April is startled and accidentally makes it rain! "Oh dear," Rupert sighs. "The ink has run. Now we'll never be able to read the label . . ."

"I'm so sorry," April cries. "I didn't mean to soak you or ruin the label!" Rupert knows that April is telling the truth, and he comforts her. "Look, there's my friend Bingo. He's the cleverest chum I have. Maybe he'll help us?" Bingo is a brainy pup and loves to figure things out, he studies the address label carefully. "There's a few letters I can still read . . . that one must be a 'B' . . . leave it with me!" he says confidently.

RUPERT GETS A FRIGHT

They leave the pup to contemplate,
And move on, while it's not too late.

They cross the woods. They're almost through,
When someone jumps out, shouting, "Boo!"

"It's only us," sneers Ferdy Fox.
"Now tell me, what's that in your box?"

But this time, April's ready too.
She soaks the foxes! "Go, now. Shoo!"

Rupert thanks Bingo. "We'll take this parcel to the post office in the meantime," he decides, as they leave the pup behind to puzzle over the label. Rupert and April make their way through the woods together. Rupert is just asking April what time she thinks it is, when they hear footsteps behind them. "W-w-what was that?" Rupert asks. He looks around but can't see anyone. Then suddenly, someone shouts out, "Boo!"

Rupert jumps, dropping the parcel, and two voices start laughing. Out pop Freddy and Ferdy Fox, the troublesome fox twins. "It's only us," Ferdy sneers. "Yeah, scared you, didn't we?" Freddy adds. Rupert has caught his breath by now, and reaches down to pick up the fallen parcel. "What's in the box?" Ferdy asks. "If it's something nice like sweets, we'll take it." This annoys April Showers. "It's not your parcel!" she calls and gives the foxes a good soaking!

RUPERT'S MYSTERY IS SOLVED

Although a lot of time has passed,
The post office appears at last!

"We'd like to pass this parcel on,"
Says Rupert, "But the label's gone."

But just then, Bingo rushes in,
His face in an enormous grin!

"I've solved it," Bingo tells the pair.
"This parcel is for . . . Mr Bear!"

"Thank you," Rupert says to April. "I guess *sometimes* it's helpful to drench someone." Rupert and April travel the rest of the way to the Nutwood Post Office without any more disruptions. It's been quite an adventure, but fortunately the post office is still open! Rupert shows the postman the parcel and explains how the label must have fallen off on Nutwood Common before the Spring Imps found it. "Can you help us find the owner?" he asks.

The postman is just about to answer, when the door swings open and Bingo rushes in. "I've solved it!" the little pup gasps. "I ran all the way here after you. The capital letters and the gaps between them . . . I believe the parcel is addressed to Mr Bear!" "Yes, that's just what I was going to say," the postman laughs. "It must have fallen out somehow. Thank you for finding it!" Rupert is almost too surprised to speak. "After all that, it's for my daddy?" he stutters.

RUPERT SURPRISES HIS MUMMY

The problem's solved! The bear's so glad,
He takes his friend to meet his dad.

Cries Mr Bear, "You've helped my plants!
And found my parcel – what a chance!"

His mummy can't believe her eyes.
"The missing jigsaw piece!" she cries.

"My jigsaw puzzle is complete!"
Cheers Mrs Bear. "Oh, what a feat!"

"I'd better take it home with me," Rupert says. He asks April Showers to come back with him and meet his parents. April is thrilled to be invited! When they arrive at Rupert's house, Mr Bear is in the garden. "Let me help you," April says generously, and waters all of Mr Bear's plants with her rain cloud. Mr Bear is very grateful! And he's even more surprised when Rupert shows him the parcel and explains how they came to find it.

"This parcel is a surprise that I ordered for your mummy," Mr Bear says. "What is it?" Rupert asks. "Well, it's a surprise," Mr Bear laughs. They take it inside to Mrs Bear, who opens it at once. "Why . . . it's the missing puzzle piece!" she cries. "I wrote to the jigsaw company and ordered a replacement for you," Mr Bear replies, his eyes twinkling. "Now you can finish your jigsaw!" Rupert says to his delighted mummy.

RUPERT SAYS GOODBYE TO APRIL

They shower April with their thanks.
She vows to give up all her pranks.

"I'm so glad that we met today,"
Says April. "Now I'm on my way."

With April's rain, the flowers grow,
And bloom, under a big rainbow!

And Rupert cheers, "Your rain will bring,
The most amazing Nutwood Spring!"

Mrs Bear looks out of the window. "Oh, look at the garden!" she cries. For April's showers have made the plants flourish. "You know," Rupert begins, "You could do a lot more with your rain cloud than just play pranks on people." "I won't play tricks any more!" says April. "Well, most of the time at least." Rupert laughs, thinking about Freddy and Ferdy. "I must be off now," April says, and Rupert offers to walk with her back to the Spring Imps.

Rupert and April say goodbye to Mr and Mrs Bear. They cross over Nutwood Common again. Every few steps, April snaps her fingers and the little cloud sprinkles raindrops over the grass. Rupert sees more daffodils, crocuses and violets pop up. "It's so colourful," he cheers, "almost like a rainbow." "A rainbow?" April says. "That's a wonderful idea!" She spreads her arms wide, and a bright rainbow appears. "What an amazing Nutwood Spring we're going to have!" Rupert cries. THE END.

Spot the Difference

It's a beautiful spring day and Rupert and his pals are having lots of fun. There are 9 differences between the two pictures. Can you spot them all?

32

RUPERT
and the
SECRET PATH

Constable Growler is far from pleased when he discovers what
Bingo has used to make the way to his hide-out. But later on, by
accident, Rupert lays a more useful trail which leads the policeman
to solve a big mystery.

RUPERT'S CHUM IS PUZZLED

"There's Sara! What's she looking at?"
And Rupert runs to have a chat.

The puzzled little girl has found
A line of sand, strewn on the ground.

"Perhaps it leaked out from a sack,"
Says Rupert, "and it made a track."

"Oh, no! It's been put down with care,
In little handfuls, here and there."

WHILE walking past the trees one day Rupert spies a small figure further inside the wood. "Surely that's Sara from the other end of the village," he thinks. "What is she looking at?" He calls, "Hi Sara, have you found something?" "Hello Rupert, come and see this," she says in a puzzled voice. "What is it?" asks Rupert, as he joins her. "Why, it's only a line of sand on the grass. What's wrong with that?" "Well, where is it from?" says Sara. "There are no sand pits in these parts and we are nowhere near the seashore." Sara is still puzzled. "This little line of sand wasn't here yesterday," she says. "How did it come?" "Who knows?" says Rupert. "Perhaps somebody walked this way with a leaky bag of sand." Again, Sara shakes her head. "No, that won't do," she declares. "If that happened the sand would be in a thin line, but it isn't. It's in blobs or small handfuls. It looks as if it's been put down on purpose by someone. But who? And why?"

RUPERT KEEPS ON THE TRAIL

"Let's follow it! We'd better go
In opposite directions, though."

Upon the grass, so fresh and green,
A track of sand is clearly seen.

A face peeps from a leafy clump,
"Why, Bingo! How you made me jump!"

"You've found my secret path! But how?
No one has seen me, up till now!"

Rupert began to find Sara's problem more interesting. "You're quite right. What a detective you are!" he says. "Some of the little handfuls of sand are a yard apart. If they have put them down on purpose somebody must be making a private track." "Oo, that's exciting!" says Sara. "Shall we follow it and see where it leads?" "Well, we don't know which way it's going," says Rupert. "We'd better try in opposite directions." Sara agrees and they move off. The sand track leads Rupert into very heavy undergrowth. "This gets more and more puzzling," he mutters. "Who would want to make a track right into the densest part of the wood?" All at once he hears someone near him. Next minute the face of his pal Bingo, the brainy pup, appears just ahead. "How on earth did you get here, Rupert?" says Bingo. "I was following a sand track," begins Rupert, "and . . ." "What!" Bingo interrupts. "D'you mean to say you've followed my secret path?"

RUPERT IS SHOWN A SAND BIN

"But, Bingo, nobody could pass,
And not see sand strewn on the grass!"

"Let's go back to the other end,"
Sighs Bingo, "where you sent your friend."

A sand bin stands across a road,
He says, "That's where I get each load."

"Where's Sara? Did she lose her trail?
Let's find her, when you've filled your pail."

Rupert stares at the brainy pup. "Why do you call it a secret path?" he asks. "The sand's clear and bright. Anyone can see it. Sara spotted it at once and saw that it wasn't there by accident." "Oh dear, I never realised that," says Bingo, gloomily. "I can't be as brainy as I thought I was! Anyway, why isn't Sara on the path too?" "She is," Rupert replies. "Only she went the opposite way to find the other end." "Then let's follow," says Bingo. "And I'll show you where I got the sand."

The small blobs of sand are quite clear and Bingo trots along at a good pace. "You must have been working hard to make so much of a track using only that little pail," says Rupert. "Yes, I had to keep at it, but it was interesting," says Bingo, as they reach the edge of the wood, "and that's where I fetched it from." He points to an iron sand bin and begins to refill the pail. "Where's Sara?" asks Rupert. "She must've seen the bin. Why didn't she come back to tell me?"

RUPERT FEELS VERY SHAKY

The policeman steps out, stern and gruff,
"I've sent her home! Put down that stuff!"

"Why are you taking Council sand?
You'll bring it back, d'you understand?"

"Scrape up that sand path, inch by inch,
And tip it back, yes, every pinch!"

The chums then start to scrape and scratch,
To gather up each sandy patch.

Before the two pals can worry about Sara, they are startled by the sudden appearance of a large figure who has been hiding behind a tree. "Never mind about young Sara," says the gruff voice of Constable Growler. "And I've been waiting to catch the rascals who have been stealing sand. Now I've got 'em. I never thought it would be *you* two." "Oh dear, I am sorry!" quavers Bingo. "Is it your sand?" "No, 'tis Council sand," growls the Constable. "Why do *you* want it?"

Bingo looks frightened. "I wanted the sand to make a little path," he says. "Ho, did you!" says Constable Growler. "Well, that sand is wanted for the Queen's roads, not Bingo's roads, so just you return that pailful and then go and bring back what you took away, and look sharp about it." Feeling very shaky, the little pals returned to the wood. "I say, I'm sorry to bring you into this," says Bingo. "You were a sport not to tell him that I was the only one to blame."

RUPERT AND BINGO ARE WEARY

"Oh dear," exclaims the brainy pup,
"We'll never get it all scooped up!"

They bring some full pails back at length,
But Bingo gasps, "I've no more strength!"

"Your secret path ends there, just look!"
Calls Rupert from a mossy nook.

Asks Rupert, now their work is done,
"Why make a path, a secret one?"

Rupert and Bingo find the work is very slow. "Oh dear," says Bingo at length, flopping back against a tree. "It was easy enough to drop little pinches of sand, but it's almost impossible to pick them up again out of the grass. I got tired enough making the path. This sort of work is worse. I feel almost dead!" However, they go on scraping and take some full pails back. "It's no good," groans Bingo at last. "This sand bin will never be as full as it was however hard we try!" Although getting more and more tired Rupert and Bingo keep on working. All at once Rupert gives a cry. "Look, your secret path seems to end here," he calls. "Yes," answers Bingo. "That's as far as I had made it when you met me. You *have* been a good pal. This wasn't your fault. You might have just gone home." "Oh well, now we can go home together as there's no more sand track," laughs Rupert. Then he gives a start. "Hi, wait," he cries, "you mustn't leave me yet!"

RUPERT CRAWLS UNDER BUSHES

"You've helped me, Rupert! In return,
My well-kept secret you shall learn."

"My path," says Bingo, "would have led
Beneath this bush. Now mind your head."

Around a low tree Rupert crawls,
And finds a ruin with thick walls.

First, round a corner Bingo peeps,
Then through a doorway softly creeps.

Bingo gazes at Rupert. "Well, what's the idea now?" he asks. "Have you thought of something new?" "No, not new," Rupert chuckles. "It's the most important question of all. You went to an awful lot of trouble making a secret path. Why did you do it? Was it going to lead anywhere?" Bingo ponders awhile. "That's a secret, too," he murmurs. "But now you've a right to share it. Come, I'll show you where the last bit of the path would have led." He dives right under a low bush.

Wondering where his pal can possibly be leading, Rupert crawls after him under the bush, then under another one and round a low tree, and at length he catches up with him. "Here we are, this is what I've found." Bingo's voice has sunk to a whisper. "Be careful how you go." In front of him Rupert sees a mass of weeds and brambles surrounding the remains of an old building made of large blocks. Signaling Rupert to be silent, Bingo peeps around a corner. Then he moves faster.

RUPERT EXPLORES THE PLACE

"This is my private hide-out, yes!
So, keep your voice down, none must guess!"

"My staircase is these broken blocks,
Come on, it's just like climbing rocks!"

An open space leads from the gloom
Into a sunlit upper room.

Says Bingo, "Where that wall has been,
The trees have formed a leafy screen."

Bingo leads the way through an opening without a door and Rupert finds himself in what was a room. In one corner is a heap of broken blocks from an upper wall that has collapsed. "Why are you being so quiet?" whispers Rupert. "Who do you expect to find here?" "Nobody," Bingo murmurs. "That's just the point!" "What point?" says Rupert in surprise. "Why, don't you see?" breathes Bingo. "I want this place kept secret. If we're heard people in other parts of the wood might become too inquisitive." While he has been speaking so quietly Bingo has clambered up the pile of blocks and rubble and, still wondering, Rupert climbs after him. At the top he sees a space of daylight and pulling himself through he finds himself in an odd-shaped upper room. One outer wall has fallen away, but it has been replaced by a mass of branches and leaves from trees growing below. 'It's a lovely place to have found," says Rupert. "Will you invite our pals here too?"

RUPERT REACHES A HIDE-OUT

"My hide-out is for working in,"
The pup tells Rupert with a grin.

"This new fuse-powder, when it's lit,
Burns silently! Let's try a bit!"

"There, isn't that a lovely flame!"
Beams Bingo. "Aren't you glad you came?"

Then, "Hush," he breathes, "it's time we went,"
And they begin the rough descent.

Bingo grins at Rupert. "Now that I've found this wonderful quiet hide-out I don't want any other pals to know about it, so you mustn't say a word," he says. "Then what *do* you mean to do here?" says Rupert. "Hush! Not so loud," pleads Bingo. "I mean this place to be for work. You know my hobby, experimenting with new gadgets and things. Well, the Professor has given me a wonderful new fuse-powder and this satchel's chock full of it." Rupert gazes in curiosity at the satchel. "It doesn't make any noise," whispers Bingo, "so there's no reason why you shouldn't see what it looks like." There is a large, flat bowl on the shelf and into it he pours some of the new fuse-powder. "The Professor has shown me how to light it safely," he explains. "Now stand back a bit, and I'll light the edge. There! Isn't that a lovely colour?" In a moment the powder has all burned, the smoke has drifted away, and Rupert and Bingo silently creep down to the floor below.

41

RUPERT CALLS BINGO BACK

Outside, he pauses, tense and glum,
"Ssh! Rupert! Which way did we come?"

The pals prowl round for quite a while,
Then Rupert beckons with a smile.

"There's still some sand left, quite a lot!
And here's your pail!" Then off they trot.

The faint track leads them through the trees,
Says Bingo, "Keep my secret, please!"

Outside the building Bingo seems nervous again. "Don't be scared," breathes Rupert. "I can't hear a sound. There's nobody about." After a few minutes Bingo stops altogether. "I do wish these bushes weren't so thick and muddled," he says. "I found my way in, but I can't remember how to get back!" They push through the undergrowth and suddenly Bingo sees Rupert waving and beckoning, not daring to shout. Bingo reaches Rupert. "What's up? What have you found?" he says

quietly. "Why, look, it's your secret path!" whispers Rupert excitedly. "There's lots of sand in the grass that we couldn't possibly pick up. It's still easy to see it." All Bingo's nervousness goes at once. He trots along the track until he finds his pail. "Here's another way out of the wood," he smiles. "Yes, and thank goodness we needn't whisper anymore!" says Rupert. "But we part here," says Bingo. "I'm going the other way. Goodbye, don't tell anyone about my secret."

RUPERT DOES NOT STAY LONG

A gentle voice bids Rupert stop,
It's Sara, heading for a shop.

Thinks Rupert Bear, "I must not tell
About that ruin in the dell."

Instead, he tells how they were made
To scrape the sand up from the glade.

His story finished, off he goes,
But Sara's puzzled, Rupert knows.

Rupert hurries homeward round the edge of the wood. "Hi Rupert, just a minute," calls a voice, and his pal Sara reappears. "My mummy sent me out again on an errand," she says, "and I had to come this way to see if you were still about. I found where that sand came from, but Constable Growler sent me home. What did *you* find?" "I – I found Bingo," says Rupert. "He was making the track." "Why?" asks Sara. "Where was it leading?" Rupert hesitates. "Oh dear," he thinks. "This is going to be difficult!" Remembering his promise to keep Bingo's secret, Rupert thinks quickly how much to tell Sara. "The track wasn't quite finished," he says. "I found Bingo and went back with him to that bin, but Constable Growler caught us! He told us he had sent you home and made us pick up the sand on the track. It was awful and made us very tired. And now, please, I must go." And before Sara can ask any more awkward questions he says, "Goodbye, Sara, see you soon," and runs off.

RUPERT GLIMPSES A STRANGER

The little bear decides, next day,
To run to school a shorter way.

Across his path a figure streaks,
From patch to patch of wood he sneaks.

"That man is new to me, I think,
How stealthily he seems to slink!"

Then Rupert spies, as he turns round,
A scrap of paper on the ground.

Rupert tells his story to Mr and Mrs Bear without saying where Bingo's secret path has led, and his efforts in picking up sand have made him so tired that he is glad to go to bed. Next morning he is fresh again and starts off in good time for school. Taking his usual shortcut over part of the Common he notices somebody moving rapidly from one patch of woodland to another. "Hello, that doesn't look like anybody belonging to the village," he thinks. "Who can he be? And why is he in such a hurry?" He is careful to keep out of sight as the man crosses a ridge. "Oh dear," mutters Rupert. "I do wonder who that stranger is. I'm sure I've never seen him before. Why is he walking through the woods instead of out here on the Common?" Although it takes him out of his way, Rupert follows the man who continues to hurry through the glades. Soon the little bear realises he may be late for school. Just as he turns back, he notices a piece of crumpled paper on the ground.

RUPERT ASKS THE GIRL GUIDES

"These marks are like a diagram,
Hmm, how inquisitive I am!"

"I'll ask those Guides! They're stopping, good!
They're pointing out Pendagron Wood."

"It's well drawn," says the youngest Guide,
But what it is, they can't decide.

"Look, there's that very hush-hush place!
Some say it's for exploring space!"

Rupert picks up the crumpled paper. "That stranger just passed here," he thinks. "I wonder if he dropped it. There are a lot of marks on it, but they don't seem to mean anything. Hello, there are three of the Guides on the way to their school. I'll see if they can make head or tail of this." As Rupert hurries forward the Guides turned to greet him. "I've just picked this up," says Rupert. "Do you think it is anything important?" the three Girl Guides in their school uniforms peer at the piece of paper. "It's carefully drawn in thick pencil lines," says Janet. "Yes, but what is it?" says Beryl, the eldest. "Perhaps it's just a doodle," suggests Pauline. "Oh well, it's school time, so I mustn't wait," says Rupert. "Tell me, what were you pointing at when I came along?" "Do you see that new building in Pendragon Wood?" says Beryl. "It's terribly hush-hush. Nobody knows if it is for atom power or space rockets, and it's being built where nobody can get near it!"

RUPERT IS LATE FOR SCHOOL

Now Rupert walks on with a frown,
So deep in thought that he slows down.

The teacher snaps, "You're late for school.
How come? You're early as a rule."

He takes the little bear aside,
Then scans that paper, eyes awide!

"When school is over, please remain,
There's quite a lot you must explain."

Without trying further to understand the marks on the crumpled paper, the three Guides run off to their own school while Rupert goes on his way. Seeing some of his pals ahead of him he does not hurry and, while he puzzles over the paper, he walks more and more slowly until, arriving at the school door, he looks up with a start. "And what does this mean?" asks the schoolmaster. "Why are *you* of all people the last to arrive? You're late, Rupert. There must be a reason. Tell me what it is?" Rupert nervously says how sorry he is to be late for school and shows the piece of crumpled paper. The teacher glances at it crossly and seems about to toss it away, when he pauses and his expression changes. Looking at it more carefully he turns it one way and then another. "Tut-tut, I'm wasting time," he says at length. "To your places, all of you, we must begin school. And you, Rupert. Please don't hurry away afterwards." He now sounds suddenly quite kind.

RUPERT DRAWS THE PLAN

When Bingo asks, "What did I miss?"
The teacher calls, "I won't have this!"

"If you find more, or see that man,
Report as quickly as you can."

"The policeman! What's all this about?"
Asks Bingo, then they hurry out.

"What was that paper? Tell me, quick!"
So, Rupert draws it, with a stick.

During class Bingo whispers inquisitively to Rupert but only earns a bad mark. After school the teacher asks Rupert to tell all that has happened since he left home. "H'm, well, listen to me Rupert," he says thoughtfully. "If you see that stranger again promise that you will tell me or Constable Growler at once." "Oo, yes. Do you want me to start a search?" says Rupert eagerly. "No, just keep your eyes open," says the teacher. "That will be enough." Outside the school Bingo has lagged behind the others and seems more curious than ever to know what Rupert had found that made the teacher so interested. "It was a crumpled bit of paper," says Rupert. "It had marks on it and if I find any more I have to tell him, or Constable Growler." "What, the policeman?" exclaims Bingo. "Quick, tell me what marks were on the paper." Bending down, Rupert scratches the path with a stick. "As far as I remember, they were lines like this," he says.

RUPERT MAKES FOR THE WOOD

The brainy pup jumps to his feet,
"Early tomorrow, we must meet!"

"Come to my secret path, and wait!"
Then off he runs at such a rate.

Says Mummy, "I'll see you're awake
and give you sandwiches to take."

Next morning Rupert, with his snack,
Sets off to find the faint sand track.

To Rupert's surprise Bingo shows signs of excitement just as the school teacher did. "What's the matter?" asks the little bear. "My drawing on the path wasn't very good, but it was something like the marks on that bit of paper. Have you any idea what that crumpled paper was?" For a moment Bingo is silent, then he turns. "There's still enough sand on my secret path for us to follow it," he says urgently. "Tomorrow's a holiday, so we meet there after breakfast." Then he quickly dashes away, leaving Rupert more puzzled than ever. "Why didn't he answer my questions?" he murmurs. "And what can his secret path have to do with the crumpled paper?" After watching his pal out of sight, he hurries home and tells his mummy what Bingo wants him to do, so next morning she makes up a packet of sandwiches and he sets off again. Several of his other pals are out, including Sara, but he runs straight ahead and won't tell any of them where he is going.

RUPERT MUST BE VERY QUIET

Like golden dust that sand path gleams,
Then – Hiss! – how close that warning seems!

"What's up?" the little bear demands.
"Hush! Get right down!" his chum commands.

Rupert obeys, and now they both
Crawl slowly through the undergrowth.

"Hush, listen!" peeping from a tree,
Who but that stranger should they see!

Rupert makes his way to the edge of the wood and looks around carefully. "I wonder if I can find what's left of that secret path," he thinks. "Ah, here it is. Now where is Bingo?" The silence is suddenly broken by a loud hiss. It comes again and, moving forward, he spies his friend flat on the ground. "What on earth are you doing?" Rupert demands. "You made me jump. Why are you crawling about like that?" "Hush!" says Bingo. "Get right down. Follow me and don't make a sound!" Bingo seems so serious that Rupert does as he is told and crawls slowly after Bingo under bushes and through tall grasses. "Is this some new game?" he breathes. "No, it certainly isn't," murmurs Bingo. "Hush! Listen." And, sure enough, there is the sound of someone moving. A dark shape passes between some bushes and disappears again. Rupert gives a gasp. "I've seen him before," he whispers softly. "I don't like this. It's that mysterious stranger!"

RUPERT DISCOVERS A PAPER

*"Quick, to my hide-out! We must find
A paper scrap he left behind."*

*"I tossed it somewhere," Bingo sighs.
"It's here!" the little bear replies.*

*"Why, it's a map! This cross marked here
Is in Pendragon Wood, it's clear!"*

*"Pendragon Wood!" gasps Rupert Bear,
"That hush-hush place is built just there!"*

When the stranger is far enough away Bingo hurries to the ruined building. "You knew he was here" says Rupert. "Was that why you asked me to join you today?" "No, not altogether," mutters Bingo. "I knew *someone* had been here because I too found a scrap of paper here. I didn't know it was important until the schoolmaster was so excited about your piece. I screwed it up and threw it away somewhere. I can't remember where." "There's a bit here," calls Rupert. "Would that be it?" Bingo seizes the paper excitedly and spreads it out. "It has scribbles on it very like those that were on my piece," says Rupert. "Why ever did the teacher think they were so important?" "They look very much like a map of the roads and paths round here," says the brainy pup suddenly. "And there's a cross marked here. Let's see, that would be the middle of Pendragon Wood." "Why!" exclaims Rupert, "that's the place that Beryl was pointing at. The hush-hush building!"

RUPERT HIDES WITH HIS CHUM

"Why would that stranger make a map?"
Then Rupert hears some branches snap!

"He's coming, Bingo!" Just in time,
Into the upper room they climb.

"He can't squeeze through that space. Don't fret,"
breathes Rupert. "We're quite safe, as yet."

They cross towards that screen of trees,
"Could we get out down one of these?"

The two pals gaze at each other. "If both scraps of paper belong to that stranger, why is he sneaking about making maps?" says Bingo. "Hush, I heard a branch snap," whispers Rupert. "He may be coming back. We mustn't go out and get caught. Don't throw that piece away. Fold it and put it in your pocket and – quick – we must hide in that upper room!" Scrambling as fast as they can up the rough blocks they squeeze through the small space and now it is Rupert's turn to insist on silence. Listening anxiously the pals hear somebody below. 'We're trapped!' whispers Bingo. "Not yet," breathes Rupert. "He doesn't know we're here. And anyway he can't squeeze through that little space. Let's have a look at those trees growing across the open wall." They cross slowly and silently and look out. "We *might* get out this way," mutters Bingo, softly. "The entrance faces the other way so he wouldn't see us, but could we possibly do it quietly enough?"

RUPERT REMEMBERS THE POWDER

They share the snack, each thinking hard,
While footsteps keep them both on guard.

Says Bingo, "He could stay all day!
I'm going to try and get away."

Then Rupert thinks, "I'll just retrieve
This precious powder! Then I'll leave!"

They clamber down without a word,
Each hopes the stranger has not heard.

The two pals look doubtfully at the way down the branches. "Could we do it without being heard?" breathes Rupert, in the tiniest whisper. "It's safer to wait a bit and listen in case that stranger goes away. Let's eat the sandwiches that Mummy made for me." So, they undo the packet very slowly so as not to make the paper rustle and set to. After a time, Bingo becomes restless. "I can still hear him pottering about," he murmurs. "I'm going to try to get away." And he slips carefully on to a tree. Rupert watches anxiously as his pal descends slowly and is just going to follow when an idea strikes him. "If that man does catch us, he'll discover the upper space and then he'll find the satchel of precious powder that Bingo has brought," he thinks. "I'd better take it, and if we're caught, perhaps I can drop it into hiding." Creeping very gently back he lifts the satchel, puts the strap over his shoulder and returns. Bingo is still making his way down as silently as he can.

RUPERT'S JOURNEY IS HARD

When Rupert lands, his chum has gone,
But now a slight hiss leads him on.

From bush to bush their way they grope,
That man won't follow them, they hope.

Gasps Rupert, "How these brambles scratch!
Thank goodness here's a clearer patch!"

They leave the wood, then down they flop!
Moans Bingo, "I feel fit to drop!"

The satchel is heavier than Rupert expects, and it makes his descent of the tree more difficult. Hearing a slight thud below him, he looks down. Bingo's patience has given out at the end, and he jumps the last few feet. When Rupert reaches the ground, his pal is not in sight, but a slight hiss shows which direction he has taken. "I say, where are you going?" Rupert whispers. "Is your secret path this way?" "There's no time to bother about that," replies Bingo. "Come on, don't dawdle!"

Rupert struggles through dense undergrowth, getting scratched and breathless. "D'you know where you're going?" he asks. "Must we take such a hard way?" "That man may have heard us," says Bingo. "The harder this is for us the harder it will be for him to follow us. Look, here's an easier bit, perhaps it will lead us out of the forest." But when they reach the edge of the wood, they are so tired that they flop down on the grass. "Oh dear, I've no idea where we are now!" sighs Rupert.

RUPERT FINDS THE BAG EMPTY

"Your powder's gone! The satchel's torn!
I must have caught it on a thorn!"

Now Rupert looks round, all agog,
"Why, here comes Sara with her dog!"

"Please, could you bring the policeman here?"
He asks her. "We're too tired, I fear."

"We made the policeman rather vexed,"
Says Sara, looking quite perplexed.

After a rest the little pals prepare to move on, but when he lifts the satchel Rupert gives a start. "Oh, look!" he cries in distress. "I saved the precious fuse-powder, but there must have been a hole in the satchel. There's hardly any left." "Well, it can't be helped," sighs Bingo. "I expect the Professor will make some more one day. Now we *must* find Constable Growler." Suddenly Rupert turns and points. "There's someone coming," he cries. "Why, I believe it's Sara!" The small figure approaches, and, sure enough, it is Sara who is exercising her little dog. "Hello, Rupert," she calls. "And Bingo too! Are you looking for more sand? You *do* look tired!" "We want to find Constable Growler . . ." begins Rupert. "I saw him just now," says Sara. "If you run you'll catch him." "Oh dear, we can't run any more," says Bingo. "Would *you* fetch him?" At that Sara turns thoughtful. After what happened two days ago none of the pals wants to face the constable.

RUPERT BEGINS THE STORY

"Still, he was cross with you, not me,"
And off she runs, quick as can be.

The chums unfold that crumpled sheet,
Then comes the tramp of heavy feet.

"Our teacher told us to report,
If we found papers of this sort."

"My goodness! It's another clue!
You've seen the man we're after, too!"

After a long pause Sara makes up her mind. "The constable was angry with you, not with me," she says. "Anyway, I'm not as tired as you are so I'd better fetch him, though what you want him for I can't imagine. I hope you aren't in more trouble!" And off she runs. "We'd better make sure that the second piece of crumpled paper is safe," says Rupert. "Yes, here it is," says Bingo, taking it from his pocket and unfolding it. As they gaze at it, they hear heavy footsteps returning.

"Now then, young scamps," says Constable Growler sternly. "Sara says you want me, so here I be! What is it this time? More mischief I'll be bound." "Please, *no!*" says Rupert. "We've found something that Teacher said we must show you." "Yes, this is it," says Bingo. The constable takes the paper slowly and suspiciously, but in a moment his expression changes. "My goodness!" he gasps. "'Tis another clue. This is important and urgent. Where did you find it? And when?"

RUPERT PEERS AT THE GROUND

"Your sand track, though you did not know,
Led to his hide-out! Quick let's go!"

"Wait!" Rupert calls the little group,
And looking puzzled, back they troop.

"This leaking satchel, we shall find,
Has left a better trail behind!"

"Yes, here's some powder," Rupert grins,
"Here's where my secret path begins!"

Constable Growler wants to set to work at once as soon as he hears where the second scribbled map was found. "So that sand track of yours was leading to the very spot before you knew that it was the hide-out of the man we want to catch!" he cries. "Come on, to that sand bin. It is a long way off, right round the other side of this big wood, so we must hurry." "Oh dear," moans Bingo. "I'm too tired to go so far." As they move off Rupert has a sudden idea and at his call the others look at him curiously. "What's the matter?" asks Sara. "Don't you want another walk along Bingo's secret path?" "There's no need to go so far. At least, I don't think so if my idea is right," says Rupert. "There should now be another secret path, even more secret than the first one." "B-but *where*?" exclaims Bingo. "It's practically here!" laughs Rupert. "Let's find the exact place where we came out of the wood this time." And he begins peering at the ground carefully.

RUPERT'S PLAN IS TRIED OUT

Says Growler, frowning, "Am I right?
You need the powder set alight?"

There's first a fizz, and then a flash,
With fright the dog then makes a dash!

The powder burns along its line,
"Come on," says Rupert. "This is fine!"

Now Growler, guided by that flame,
Moves off, the way the two chums came.

Quite soon Rupert seems to find what he is looking for. "Don't you remember, Bingo?" he murmurs. "Your satchel had a hole in it and the fuse-powder leaked all the way through the wood. There's some of the powder here." "Whee-oo! I see your idea," exclaims Bingo. "Perhaps Constable Growler will light it for us." The policeman looks puzzled as he takes out his pocket lighter. "I s'pose it's alright," he says. "Though I'm not quite sure what this is about." He puts the flame of his lighter into the grass and instantly there is a fizz and a splutter, then all at once there is a brilliant flash as the powder catches light properly. Sara is pulled away by the little dog who has been frightened, but Rupert starts forward. "Come on," he says. "This will lead us to the old ruin although we came a different way." The constable, in his astonishment, asks no questions as he goes with Bingo and Rupert round corners and under bushes, guided by the burning powder.

RUPERT GIVES A WARNING

The powder burns out, with a fizz,
"Well, show me where your ruin is!"

Then Rupert whispers, with a thrill,
"There's someone moving! Keep quite still!"

A figure passes, dark and grim,
"The stranger!" Rupert breathes. "That's him!"

"He's gone! He won't get very far,
Now, where's his hide-out? Here we are!"

As the little party work their winding way through the wood they keep very quiet. "If the man we're after is still in your old ruin, he mustn't hear us," murmurs Constable Growler. All at once the fizzing powder gives a last spurt and goes out. "Oh dear, I expect you caught the satchel on a thorn and it began leaking just here," whispers Bingo. "I can't remember how we arrived at this point." They look around for clues. All at once Rupert stiffens. "Hold still a minute," he breathes.

"There's someone moving." At Rupert's warning the others stand very still. Keeping well in the cover, and peeping through the leaves, they see a dark figure passing through the undergrowth. "Are you going to catch him now?" whispers Rupert. Constable Growler waits until the mysterious figure is well away from them. "All in good time," he mutters. "Let's find where he came from." Almost at once they find the ruin and after a careful look round to see that all is quiet, they enter.

RUPERT STARES AT THE CASE

Inside, the policeman's voice is tense,
"Now I must search for evidence!"

"That man's a spy, we're pretty sure!
But I need proof! Ah, what's that for?"

The policeman lifts a slab of wood,
"That leather case – it means no good!"

"That man is dangerous, indeed!
These papers are the proof I need!"

"Now then," says Constable Growler briskly. "So long as that stranger doesn't know that we've found his hide-out he's sure to come back. Meantime I want to have a quick search." "Well, I'm pretty sure he doesn't know about the upper room," says Rupert. "He could never get through the little space. And he doesn't seem to have left anything of his own in here." "I'm not so sure!" says Constable Growler, pointing. "What's that?" The policeman has spotted something that the little pals have missed. "That slab down there," he says, urgently. "It's been carefully covered with earth and pebbles." "Well, what about it?" says Rupert in a puzzled voice. "Let's take it up," says the constable. "Ah, there you are. 'Tisn't stone. It's wood. It's quite light." In the space under the slab is a strong leather case and seizing it eagerly Constable Growler examines a sheaf of papers inside it. "Just what I need!" he exclaims. "We've got him! Now it's proved!"

RUPERT LEARNS THE GOOD NEWS

"Run home! We'll catch him in due course,
He's wanted by the whole police force."

Then as it isn't safe to roam,
The two chums part and run straight home.

Next morning, voices in the lane
Send Rupert racing out again.

"That secret path, a clever plan,
Enabled us to catch our man!"

Outside the old ruin Constable Growler acts quickly. "That stranger's a dangerous spy," he explains quietly. "We mustn't make a noise in case he's coming back. Until we've caught him this is no place for you young people, so hurry away home. Meanwhile I'll put this case back so that he won't suspect we found it. Then I'll report the matter." The chums find their way by what remains of the sand track and separate. Both are thrilled to see the constable so excited by the discovery.

Next morning Rupert hears voices and runs to join his daddy. Sara has seen Constable Growler hurrying to Rupert's cottage and has followed inquisitively. "Well, little bear, we've got that spy!" says the officer. "I called up the Nutchester Police and, thanks to your secret path, we surrounded the place and caught him red-handed!" "Oo, topping!" cries Rupert. "Come on, Sara. We must go and tell Bingo at once. It was his secret path, not mine, that really started the whole affair!"

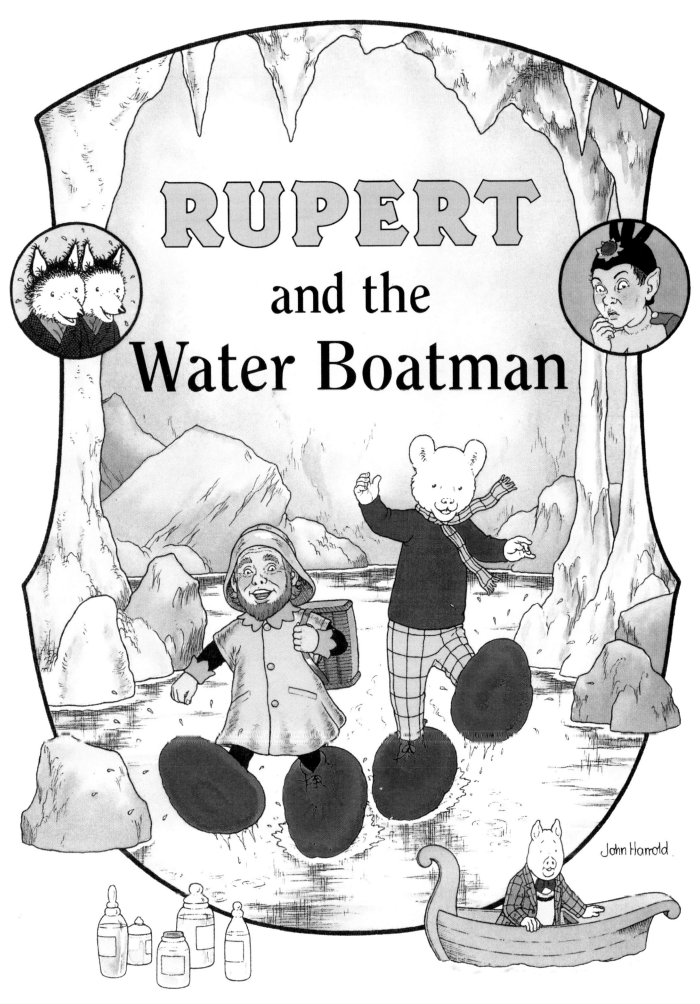

RUPERT
and the
Water Boatman

John Harrold

RUPERT HEARS A TALL STORY

A football match is underway . . .
"Let's ask the Fox brothers to play!"

But Ferdy says they're off to take
A swim in Nutwood's nice warm lake . . .

"The weather's too cold! They'll both freeze!"
Laughs Podgy. "I think it's a tease!"

The others say they think the same
And happily resume the game.

It is a chilly autumn day, Rupert and his pals are playing football together on Nutwood Common. "We could really do with a few more players!" puffs Podgy. "There are the Fox brothers," cries Rupert. "I wonder if they would like to join us?" "No, thanks," says Ferdy, when Rupert calls him over. "Normally we'd love to play, but today we're off for a swim." "A swim?" gasps Rupert. "Where?" "In the lake!" says Freddy. "It's ever so warm. We're just on our way there now . . ."

"Swimming in the lake!" laughs Podgy. "It must be some sort of joke. The water will be freezing at this time of year!" "It does seem a bit unlikely," admits Rupert. "But if the Foxes aren't really going swimming, I wonder what they're up to?" "Who knows?" shrugs Algy. "They're always playing jokes of some kind . . ." He kicks the ball high into the air and soon the chums have forgotten all about the mystery as the game carries on, with Rupert scoring the first goal.

RUPERT IS SURPRISED

Rupert is on his way home when
He sees the Fox brothers again.

They rub their fur as they walk by,
"We've got to rush home to get dry!"

Next morning Rupert's keen to see
If he can solve the mystery . . .

He nears the lake. "There's Podgy too!
"Wait!" Rupert calls. "I'll come with you."

When the chums finish playing football, it is time for Rupert to go home for tea. As he hurries across the Common, he spots the Foxes coming back from the direction of the lake. To his astonishment they are both rubbing themselves dry with their towels. "So you *did* go swimming after all!" he gasps. "Of course!" smiles Freddy. "The water was lovely and warm, even better than last time . . ." "Can't stop!" cries his brother. "We've got to get indoors before we catch a chill in this cold air."

Next morning, Rupert is still puzzled by the Foxes' strange behaviour and decides to visit the lake. He hasn't gone far when he meets Podgy, heading across the Common in the same direction. "I'm sure they're playing a trick on us!" his friend declares. "The only way to call their bluff is to find out what the lake really feels like. It's always fairly chilly, even in the summer . . ." "We'll soon find out!" says Rupert. "It's not far away, just behind those tall trees."

RUPERT FEELS THE WATER

The two chums reach the lake, which seems
So hot now that the water steams!

"A fountain!" Podgy cries. "I say!
That wasn't here the other day."

They feel the water. "Goodness me!"
It is hot! How extraordinary!"

Then Rupert notices the ground –
"Podgy! Look at these tracks I've found!"

Curious to see if the Foxes can really have gone for a swim, Rupert and Podgy hurry through the trees until they reach the edge of the lake. "I don't believe it!" gasps Rupert. "The water's steaming!" "Amazing!" blinks Podgy. "No wonder they didn't feel cold!" As the two pals stand staring at the lake, Podgy suddenly notices something even more peculiar. "There's a fountain!" he cries. "It's bubbling up out of the water." "How odd!" says Rupert. "Let's take a closer look."

Running down to the water's edge, the two pals roll up their sleeves to feel for themselves how hot it is. "Extraordinary!" cries Rupert, as he trails a hand in the water. "It's just like a warm bath!" "Perhaps we should *all* go swimming!" laughs Podgy. "The lake seems hotter now than it did in the summer." "There's definitely something odd going on," murmurs Rupert as he climbs to his feet. Then he gives a cry of surprise. "Podgy! Come and look at these strange footprints . . ."

RUPERT'S PAL FINDS A BOAT

"Come on!" he says. "Let's try to find
Whoever left this trail behind . . ."

The tracks start by the lakeside where
A pole sticks up – "There's something there!"

"A boat!" says Podgy. "Someone's stored
All sorts of little jars aboard."

"I wonder what's inside them?" he
Says. "I'll just take a look and see . . ."

"Gosh!" cries Podgy, looking at the footprints. "I wonder who made them?" "I don't know," says Rupert. "Perhaps it wasn't a *person* at all." Although they both feel rather nervous, the chums can't resist trying to find out where the footprint trail leads – and slowly start to follow them along the lakeside path. All of a sudden, Rupert stops and points to a strange sight. "There's something down by the water's edge," he whispers. "Yes," says Podgy, "but what can it be?"

"A boat!" marvels Podgy. "Someone must have moored it here while they went for a walk round the lake." "What a strange shape!" says Rupert. "It doesn't look like an ordinary rowing boat. For one thing, there aren't any oars . . ." "Look inside," says Podgy. "It's full of all sorts of bottles and jars!" "Don't touch any of them," warns Rupert, but Podgy doesn't seem to hear. "I only want to find out what's inside," he says. "You keep watch in case the owner comes back . . ."

RUPERT'S PAL IS CAST ADRIFT

*"They're all the same! But who would take
Jars of pond water from the lake?"*

*Then Podgy slips. "Oh, no!" he cries.
"I think I'm going to capsize!"*

*As Rupert looks on in dismay
The boat begins to drift away.*

*"Help!" Podgy calls. "What shall I do?"
"Don't worry! I'll keep up with you . . ."*

Stepping into the little boat, Podgy bends down and picks up one of the jars. "It's full of water!" he cries. "It looks as if it has come from the lake," says Rupert. "But who would want to collect bottles full of pond water?" "They're all the same!" says Podgy "I wonder what they're for?" "You'd better put them back before anyone sees," says Rupert. Podgy agrees, but as he leans forward the boat starts to sway from side to side. "Help!" he cries. "I've lost my balance!"

As Podgy topples backwards, he grabs wildly at an upright pole, then lands in a heap at the bottom of the boat. "Oh, no!" gasps Rupert. "It's drifting free!" Before he can do anything, the boat swings away from its mooring and begins to glide out across the lake. "What shall I do?" wails Podgy. "There aren't any oars to row back!" "Don't worry!" calls Rupert. "I'll follow you along the path. As soon as you run aground, we'll be able to pull the boat ashore."

RUPERT SEES PODGY DISAPPEAR

The boat begins to gain speed now –
"It's going by itself somehow."

Then, suddenly, it swings around
And seems about to run aground.

Poor Podgy's sure he'll hit the rock
But then he gets another shock . . .

"A cave!" gasps Rupert. "He's alright!"
Then Podgy's boat drifts out of sight.

To Rupert's surprise, the little boat seems to gather speed as it drifts out across the lake. "It's moving by itself," cries Podgy. "Impossible!" says Rupert, but as he runs along the bank the boat goes faster and faster until he can't keep up with it any longer . . . "Perhaps it's been blown by the wind," he thinks. The next moment Rupert blinks in disbelief as the boat veers off towards a rocky outcrop. "Help!" calls Podgy. "If it doesn't slow down, I'm going to crash!"

As the mysterious boat speeds through the water, it shows no sign of slowing down, but keeps on a steady path towards the rocky outcrop. "There's nothing I can do!" wails Podgy, bracing himself for the collision. Suddenly he looks up and gives a gasp of surprise. "What's happened?" calls Rupert, anxiously. "There's some sort of hidden cave!" cries Podgy. "It's covered with trailing plants." As he speaks, the boat glides silently between two rocks and disappears from sight . . .

RUPERT TRIPS OVER

"I wonder where the boat has gone?"
Thinks Rupert as he hurries on.

Then Rupert trips. Next thing he feels
Himself falling head over heels!

He clambers up, amazed to see
A stranger watching anxiously . . .

"Oh dear, my jars were in your way.
I've been collecting them all day!"

"A secret cave!" gasps Rupert. "Podgy's boat must have been carried inside by an underground stream . . ." Calling out to his chum, he runs along the path by the side of the lake as fast as he can. "I wonder if Podgy can hear me?" he thinks. "I hope he hasn't gone very far . . ." Rupert is so anxious to reach the cave that he doesn't notice a small object lying on the path. His foot hits something hard as he races along and the next moment he finds himself tumbling head over heels.

Luckily, Rupert isn't hurt by the fall. He looks up in surprise as a stranger dressed in oilskins suddenly appears. "Man overboard!" he calls. "All my fault. Didn't mean to capsize you by blocking the way with my things . . ." Helping Rupert up, he points to a small wicker basket lying on the grass. "It's full of jars and bottles," cries Rupert. "Then it must be *your* boat we saw moored by the shore." "That's right," smiles the man. "I left her there while I came to get more samples."

RUPERT ASKS ABOUT PODGY

"My friend climbed in your boat but then
It disappeared from sight again!"

"Please tell me how to bring him back!
Is there a path or special track?"

"The Waterworks is where your friend
Will come to at his journey's end."

"That's where I work. My job's to make
Reports on problems, like this lake . . ."

"Oh, dear!" sighs Rupert and tells the man how he and Podgy couldn't resist taking a closer look at the little boat. "My friend was cast adrift, then vanished into a hidden cave!" he explains. "Not to worry!" smiles the man. "My boat will have taken itself back to the Waterworks. They all do that unless there's someone to steer." "The Waterworks?" asks Rupert, as the man starts to gather his jars. "I don't understand. Who are you, and why are you collecting so many jars of water?"

"I'm a Boatman from the Waterworks!" explains the stranger. "It's our job to look after all the ponds and rivers . . . I was on my way to Nutwood to investigate a complaint from the Autumn Elves when I suddenly noticed how hot the lake was and stopped to take some samples." "It's never been like this before," says Rupert. "No," says the Boatman. "The water's hotter now than it should be in the middle of summer. Something very odd must have happened. I don't understand it at all!"

RUPERT FOLLOWS THE ELVES

Just then, two Autumn Elves appear –
"Hello! Thank goodness that you're here!"

"This way!" an Elf calls. "Follow me,
There's a door in this hollow tree . . ."

The pair are being taken to
The Autumn Elves' secret H.Q.

"It isn't far now – through that door,
The Baths are what we called you for . . ."

As Rupert and the Boatman gaze at the lake, a shrill voice calls out, "There you are! Our chief was beginning to think you weren't coming . . ." "Autumn Elves!" gasps Rupert. "Sorry to keep you waiting," says the Boatman. "We'd better set off straight away." "Can I come too?" asks Rupert? "Of course," says his new friend. "I'll take you to see the Waterworks too." "This way!" calls the second Elf. His companion hurries to a nearby tree and pulls open a hidden door . . .

Inside the tree is a steep flight of steps which leads down to a rocky tunnel. "This must be the way to the Elves' Headquarters!" whispers Rupert. "Follow me, please!" the first Elf calls to the Boatman. "The Chief should be waiting for us in the Bathhouse. He told me to take you there as soon as you arrived." "I wonder what's wrong?" thinks Rupert. "Whatever can the Boatman have to do with the Chief's bath? I thought he said he was in charge of the ponds and rivers . . ."

RUPERT HEARS WHAT IS WRONG

"Baths?" Rupert thinks. "It's a mistake.
I thought they'd noticed Nutwood's lake!"

"The bathwater from our supply
Is freezing cold! Please find out why!"

"It should be warm the whole year round,
Piped from a hot spring underground."

"I'll send you home a special way
So you can start without delay . . ."

Following the Elf through a door marked "Baths," Rupert and the Boatman find themselves face to face with the Chief Elf. "Thank goodness you've come to help us!" he cries. "I will if I can," says the man, "but what's wrong? Why have you sent for me?" "Our water!" replies the Chief. "It's normally nice and warm, direct from an underground spring, but yesterday it suddenly turned icy cold. Feel for yourself! The baths are so chilly that we've had to stop using them!"

"Good gracious!" cries the Boatman. "You're quite right, the water feels freezing! I can't think what's happened – it's piped here straight from the spring!" "What can you do?" asks Rupert. "Nothing till I know what's wrong!" declares the Boatman. 'I'll have to go back to Headquarters and ask for help. Somebody there might know all about it . . ." "But that could take ages!" sighs the Chief Elf. "I know! There's a shortcut you can travel back to the Waterworks by railcar . . ."

RUPERT RIDES IN A RAILCAR

"Our railway has a special track –
A railcar will soon take you back."

The pair climb on and find that they
Are quickly speeding on their way.

The car goes fast, then faster still,
It twists and turns its way downhill.

Then, at the far end of the line,
Rupert spots a "Waterworks" sign.

Rupert knows that the Autumn Elves have a special railway, with little cars that run along underground tracks. "There's a branch line that will take you all the way to the Waterworks!" the Chief declares. "All you have to do is keep the lever pressed forward until you want to stop . . ." Rupert and the Boatman climb into the railway car and are soon ready to start. "Good luck!" calls the Elf as Rupert pushes on the lever. "I hope you'll soon be able to find out what's gone wrong."

At first, the Elves' railcar glides along quite gently, then it veers off down a narrow turning and suddenly gathers speed. "Hold on tight!" calls the Boatman. "It's like a roller-coaster!" Our H.Q. is deep underground . . ." Eventually the car begins to slow. "We must be nearly there," says the Boatman. Sure enough, Rupert spots the end of the line and a sign reading, "Waterworks". "This way," says the Boatman. "Follow me!"

RUPERT SEES THE WATERWORKS

"This way!" the Boatman calls. They take
A pathway to a hidden lake . . .

"The Waterworks!" his guide declares
As Rupert stands amazed and stares.

The Boatman says, "You'll need a pair
Of our special pond-skates to wear . . ."

"They're what all Water Boatmen use –
Just slip them on over your shoes!"

Carefully closing the door behind him, the Boatman leads Rupert along a rocky tunnel until they reach an enormous underground lake. "There!" he says proudly, pointing to the far side. "That's the Waterworks you can see, straight ahead. Lots of streams and rivers start from here so it's the perfect spot to keep an eye on them all." "But how are we going to get across the lake?" asks Rupert. "There aren't any bridges and there don't seem to be any boats!"

"Crossing a lake is easy!" laughs the Boatman. "All you need is a pair of skates . . ." "Skates?" asks Rupert. "But it's not frozen. There isn't any ice!" "Pond-skates!" declares the Boatman, reaching into his basket. "You blow them up like water-wings, then wear them on your feet." "Wonderful!" cries Rupert. "But how am I going to get across?" "The same way!" smiles the Boatman. "I always carry a spare set, in case of emergencies. You put these on while I blow up the others . . ."

RUPERT USES POND SKATES

"Now we can both cross easily.
I'll lead the way, just follow me!"

"What fun!" laughs Rupert as they stride
Across the pond to the far side.

Two guards come out to meet the pair
And ask the Boatman who is there . . .

"A land-dweller! He's come ashore
To find someone he's looking for."

As soon as they are both ready, the Water Boatman steps out from the shore on to the surface of the lake. "Don't worry!" he calls to Rupert. "As long as you're wearing pond-skates it's easy to walk across to the other side . . ." Rupert steps out cautiously and begins to follow his friend. "You're right!" he laughs. "It's like walking on a giant sheet of glass!" "Not much further now," says the Boatman. "As soon as we reach the Waterworks, I'll take you inside."

No sooner have Rupert and the Water Boatman stepped ashore, then two guards come hurrying towards them. "Who's this?" they ask. "A land-dweller," says the Boatman. "He's searching for a missing friend . . ." "That must be the stranger who arrived earlier!" says the guard. "He told us some yarn about Nutwood lake being warm!" "It's true!" exclaims the Boatman. "And there's a new fountain, right in the middle! Come with me," he tells Rupert. "I'll take you to see your friend."

RUPERT FINDS PODGY

"Your friend's quite safe! Let's go and tell
The Inspector we're here as well . . ."

"Thank goodness you've come!" Podgy cries.
"They're all convinced I'm telling lies!"

"You say the lake's hot? Then it's true!
But why? And what are we to do?"

The Elves have cold bathwater now.
Their hot spring's warmed the lake somehow . . .

Inside the Waterworks, a maze of tunnels leads to a door marked "Head Office". "This is where we'll find your friend," the Boatman tells Rupert. "He's been taken to see the Inspector . . ." Pushing it open, he announces their arrival. "*Another* land-dweller!" gasps the Inspector. "Yes," says the Boatman. "He has come from Nutwood, with important news!" "Rupert!" cries Podgy. "Thank goodness you're here! Nobody believes the lake is hot – they all think I'm making it up!"

When the inspector hears Rupert's story, he admits that Podgy must be telling the truth . . . "I still don't understand," he complains. "*Why* has the lake grown so warm? It's never happened before." Rupert suddenly thinks he knows the answer . . . "Of course!" he cries. "The lake's not the only thing that's changed temperature. While it's got warm, the Elves' baths have turned freezing cold!" "That's right!" says the Boatman. "Their hot water must be escaping into the lake!"

RUPERT RIDES IN A SUBMARINE

"A broken pipe! We'll send a team
To mend it in a submarine . . ."

"Wait!" calls the Boatman. "Extra crew!
My friends and I are going too."

The Boatman says they'll take the same
Way to Nutwood that Podgy came.

"We're back on Nutwood's lake once more,
But where's the leak we're looking for?"

"If the Elves' hot water is escaping, there must be a broken pipe!" declares the Inspector. "I'll summon a repair team straight away . . ." "Come on!" says the Boatman. "If we hurry, we should be in time to join in. You two discovered what was wrong, so it's only fair you should see what happens next! Following him back to the lake, the pals spot a strange boat, with a diver perched on the back, "A submarine!" gasps Rupert. "Extra crew members!" the Boatman calls. "They're coming with us!"

As soon as Rupert and Podgy are safely aboard, the Boatman pulls down a glass cover and switches on the engine. "Very useful for underwater repairs!" he chuckles. "A submarine like this can go anywhere . . ." Making their way through the rocky cavern, they eventually reach a narrow opening, which leads to Nutwood lake. "As soon as we've mended the pipe, everything should go back to normal," explains the Boatman. "The only problem now is to find out where it's broken . . ."

RUPERT GOES UNDERWATER

"The fountain!" Rupert cries. "You see?
That's where the broken pipe must be!"

The submarine dives down to take
A closer look beneath the lake . . .

The pondweed sways before their eyes –
"We've found it!" everybody cries.

The diver says that he can make
A new join that will mend the break.

"The fountain!" cries Rupert. "Perhaps that's where the pipe's broken? It wasn't here before the lake grew hot . . ." "Good idea!" says the Boatman. "We'll try there first." Signalling to the diver, he presses a button on the control panel which sends the submarine plunging below the surface of the lake. "Gosh!" says Rupert. "It looks so different down here . . ." "Yes," smiles the Boatman. "Land-dwellers are always surprised! If you spot anything odd, we'll take a closer look . . ."

Before long, Rupert notices some strands of pondweed swaying from side to side. "It's the start of the fountain!" he cries. "And look, there's the broken pipe!" "Well done!" says the Boatman. "We'll drop anchor here, while the diver gets to work . . ." Climbing down from his seat, the little diver studies the pipe carefully. Opening his tool box, he takes out a spanner and fits the two pieces together. "Bravo!" cheers the Boatman. "Everything will soon be back to normal."

RUPERT SAYS GOODBYE

*"All done!" he signals. "Good as new!
Now I'll ride back again, with you . . ."*

*The submarine starts up once more
And heads towards the Nutwood shore.*

*"Goodbye! Thank you for all you've done!"
The pals both say that it was fun.*

*"The Foxes won't believe it when
They come to have a swim again!"*

When he has finished, the diver turns to the pals and signals that he is ready to go. "Excellent!" says the Boatman. "We'll cast off as soon as he's back on board." The submarine's engine gives a gentle hum and they rise slowly to the surface of the lake. "It will still feel warm for a while," says the Boatman. "But by this time tomorrow, the whole lake should be back to its proper temperature. The Elves' baths should be back to normal too!" he chuckles. "By now they'll be piping hot!"

"Thanks for all your help!" says the Water Boatman as the two pals step ashore. "We would never have been able to solve the mystery without you." "It was nothing really," says Rupert. "But I did enjoy seeing the Waterworks . . ." "I say!" chuckles Podgy. "Do you think Freddy and Ferdy will try swimming in the lake again tomorrow?" "I wonder?" smiles Rupert. "They'll certainly get a surprise if they jump in without testing the water first!"

THE END

HOW TO MAKE RUPERT'S YACHT

Here is a neat little sailing-boat needing only half a dozen folds. It was invented by a famous Japanese writer and paper-folder, Mrs Toshié Takahama, who hopes that Rupert and his pals will enjoy making it.

Take a square of paper coloured on one side and fold it once from corner to corner. Open out and fold the top lefthand edge along the sloping dotted line in Fig. 1 so that the edge stops short of the middle line (Fig. 2). Bring the righthand point right over (Fig. 3) and take it back again by the dotted line shown so that the new edge just covers the edge on Fig. 2. That makes the mainsail (Fig 4.). Bend the bottom of the sail backwards along the new dotted line and finish that fold neatly downward (Fig. 5).

Now lift the bottom edge of the figure using yet another dotted line so that the edge lies exactly along the bottom edge of the foresail (Fig. 6). Finally take the bottom point backward along the last dotted line so that the finished boat looks like Fig. 7. Press the last folds firmly.

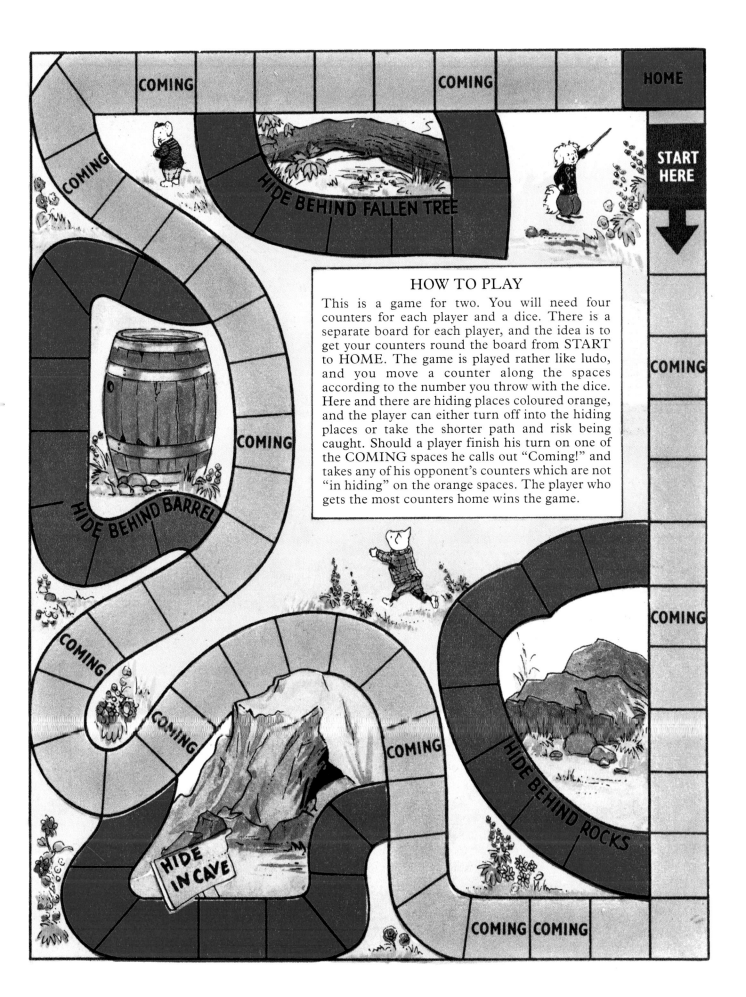

COMING

COMING

HOME

START HERE

COMING

HIDE BEHIND FALLEN TREE

COMING

COMING

COMING

HIDE BEHIND BARREL

HOW TO PLAY

This is a game for two. You will need four counters for each player and a dice. There is a separate board for each player, and the idea is to get your counters round the board from START to HOME. The game is played rather like ludo, and you move a counter along the spaces according to the number you throw with the dice. Here and there are hiding places coloured orange, and the player can either turn off into the hiding places or take the shorter path and risk being caught. Should a player finish his turn on one of the COMING spaces he calls out "Coming!" and takes any of his opponent's counters which are not "in hiding" on the orange spaces. The player who gets the most counters home wins the game.

COMING

COMING

COMING

COMING

HIDE BEHIND ROCKS

HIDE IN CAVE

COMING COMING

81

RUPERT and the SILENT DOG

"Look at that dog!" cries Rupert Bear,
"He's shopping in the store, just there."

The clever dog runs up a hill,
"Let's follow him awhile," says Bill.

Rupert and Bill have had a long walk to a neighbouring village. Having been there only a few times before, they do not know the place very well, so they are having a good look round. They find the village store almost empty, but to their surprise see a large dog with a sort of belt to which are attached two leather bags. "Look at that dog, Bill," whispers Rupert, "have you seen anything like it?" Bill doesn't answer immediately, for at that moment the dog has placed a basket in front of the shopkeeper.

The man bends down and picks up a written list and, after studying it, he loads up the leather bags and the basket with groceries. At last, satisfied that he has missed nothing, he takes the money and places the change in the basket. As soon as he has heard the coins slide into the accustomed place, the dog solemnly lifts the basket and walks straight past the pals and rapidly sets off up a slope. "What a wonderful creature he is," says Bill. "Come on, Rupert, let's follow and see where he goes to."

RUPERT AND BILL ON THE TRAIL

A heavy shower begins to fall.
They cannot see the dog at all.

The chums seek shelter from the rain,
And there they meet the dog again.

They speak to him – he pays no heed,
But just looks very fierce indeed.

The rain stops suddenly once more,
And off the dog goes, as before.

Rupert is as inquisitive as Bill. "I certainly would like to know where he is going and who he belongs to," he says. They hurry up the slope, but as soon as they reach the high ground a sharp shower of rain begins. "We've missed him," says Bill. "He has disappeared. Let's take shelter for a minute." As they push into a thick bush they realize that a pair of serious eyes are fixed on them. "It's the dog! He's sheltering with us," cries Rupert. "Good doggie! Where are you going? Whose are you?"

The dog keeps quite silent and does not move. "Let's see if he has a name on his collar," says Rupert, edging forward, but at that the strange animal turns his head ever so slightly, his eyes narrow and his top lip curls up menacingly, though he still does not make a sound. The two pals draw back hurriedly. "He looks as if he'll bite," says Bill shakily. However, nothing happens. The shower soon stops and the dog, picking up his basket, leaves the bushes and walks sedately away.

RUPERT SHELTERS HIS PAL

"I think we'd better go," says Bill,
But Rupert wants to follow still.

So on they go, until they find,
The dog has stopped, with rocks behind.

But now they have a nasty shock,
The dog dives at them from a rock.

Bill tumbles over in his fright,
But Rupert stops the dog's mad flight.

When the dog has gone Bill thinks it's time to go home. "He doesn't seem to like us," he says. "He didn't wag his tail." "No, but he didn't growl either," answers Rupert. "I'm still too inquisitive about him. He's such a clever creature." So they push on up the hill to where the surface becomes very rough. "Look!" cries the little bear, "the dog can't get any farther. There are only tall rocks beyond him." As he speaks the dog turns his head and gazes at them from behind a boulder.

Next moment the dog lowers his basket and without the slightest warning doubles round the boulder and bears down on them at a great rate. "Look out, he's coming for us!" gasps Bill. Turning to run he trips over a stone and falls headlong. Rupert sees that his pal is down and, with no time to think, steps across to shield him. The dog, taken by surprise, skids violently to a halt and for an instant they face each other. Meanwhile Bill is able to scramble to his feet.

RUPERT DECIDES TO EXPLORE

The strange dog leans towards the bear,
Then waves his front paw in the air.

"Well!" Rupert gasps, "I'm going on.
I really must know where he's gone."

The dog has disappeared again,
But there's one path that's quite plain.

A dark cave opens on the right,
But still the dog is not in sight.

After a short pause the strange dog leans his head towards the little bear and again his top lip curls up hardly showing his teeth. Then with a wave of his paw he returns to pick up his basket. "Whew, what an escape!" cries Bill. "Come, let's run." But Rupert stares in perplexity. "He really is the oddest creature," he says. "I declare he was grinning at me that time! I simply must find out where he's going." He climbs cautiously to the boulder while Bill follows very gingerly.

Beyond the boulder Rupert finds himself in a rough passage with more boulders on one side and higher rocks on the other. Just before the passage comes to a dead end, he spies a dark tunnel on the right. "The dog must have gone in there," he murmurs, "there's nowhere else for him to go." He peers in but can only see as far as the first bend. "I wish it were not all so silent," he says. "I'm going to explore it a little way. Wait for me, Bill." And in he goes on all fours.

RUPERT SENDS BILL FOR HELP

An iron door shuts behind the bear,
And he is really trapped in there.

He crawls into the larger place,
And, with the dog, comes face to face.

Now Rupert sees a man there too,
And thinks, "He'll tell me what to do."

The man looks cross and fiercely scowls,
"Why did you come in here?" he growls.

Rupert has barely reached the first bend when there is a loud clang behind him. An iron door has dropped through a slot in the rock and has shut him in. He beats on it and can faintly hear the voice of Bill beyond. "Go for help, I'm caught in here!" calls Rupert. And crawling slowly round the bend he finds he is at the entrance of a large cave while, sitting facing him, is the dog. For three minutes the dog gazes at him, silent as ever, then it turns, and Rupert can only follow.

The dog walks up to a rather untidy old gentleman who is sitting on a stool. "Oh, please, will you show me how to get out?" says Rupert nervously. "I've got shut in. I didn't mean to break into your home, if this is your home." The man gazes at him in a curious way. "Then what did you mean?" he growls. "I knew you were coming. My dog showed you as plainly as he could that he didn't want you, and still you come. Inquisitive, that's what you are, and now you must pay for it!"

RUPERT WANTS SIX LETTERS

And then he says, "I've peep-holes here,
So I can see who's coming near."

Then Rupert's asked to help the man
Complete his crossword, if he can.

He needs a word with "H" begun,
But Rupert cannot think of one.

So while the man stares at the floor,
The little bear creeps to a door.

Rupert is taken by surprise. "But please tell me," he says, "how could you know I was coming when you were sitting here?" "I have peep-holes through the rock on all sides like that one," answers the man gruffly. "I know everything that goes on. And now, no more questions. Come and help me. I'm making up a crossword and I want a word of six letters beginning with H." Feeling still more surprised Rupert kneels and sees that there are markings on a sandy part of the floor of the cave.

Getting to his feet Rupert looks round in a bewildered way. "Come on, come on," says the man harshly. "Six letters beginning with H." Rupert scratches his head and tries to think. "Oh dear, I'm not much good at spelling," he mutters, walking slowly round the cave. All at once he spies a doorway beyond an angle of rock and his hopes revive. He glances back. The man and the silent dog are intent on the crossword and do not seem to be noticing him. Gently he tries the handle.

RUPERT HEARS OF THE HERMIT

To his delight it opens wide,
And Rupert quickly slips outside.

The path ends suddenly, and so
There's no way to the rocks below.

Some birds fly round the little bear,
And ask him what he's doing there.

They say, "That man is very kind,
His little joke you must not mind."

To Rupert's great joy the door opens without a sound and ahead of him he sees another tunnel with daylight at the end of it. "This is wonderful," he breathes. "I can escape from this mad place after all!" He tiptoes forward and then stops abruptly, for below him is a steep drop. He gazes around and realizes that the tunnel is just a hole in a great cliff. There is no way of climbing either up or down. As he pauses lots of birds swoop in to look at him.

Some large birds fly round him screeching hungrily and are followed by a flock of smaller ones. "Hello," chirps a sparrow. "Who are you? You're looking pretty glum." "I'm trying to get away from that awful old man," says Rupert miserably. "Hey, don't you go calling him names!" cheeps another sparrow. "He's a lovely old man. He's a hermit and he has a dog who does all his shopping for him and he loves birds and he feeds us every day but he does like to be left alone."

88

RUPERT GIVES SIX LETTERS

"The man's a hermit," says a bird,
And Rupert thinks, "is that the word?"

"It starts with 'H', so that will do,
And there are five more letters, too."

So Rupert goes back to the man,
And speaks as bravely as he can.

The hermit looks at him awhile,
Then slowly he begins to smile.

Rupert is astonished. "Are you sure that's all true?" he asks. "Of course it is," says the sparrow. "He's even trained his dog not to bark for fear of frightening us. And he's a hermit because he wants quiet for making his crosswords. But he does love to tease people who are inquisitive. Perhaps that is why you are feeling so glum!" Rupert stares in relief. "So that explains everything!" he breathes. Then an idea strikes him. "Hermit! Surely that has six letters, and it starts with H!"

The sparrows are so sure of what they are saying that Rupert decides to go back. Re-entering the cave, he faces the old gentleman as bravely as he can. "Please, I believe you've been teasing me all the time," he says. "I'm sorry if I was inquisitive. I didn't mean any harm. And, please, is 'hermit' the word you want for your crossword?" The man and the silent dog look at him solemnly for a moment. Then they both break into a smile and the man begins to chuckle.

RUPERT HAS AFTERNOON TEA

He says, "I like you, little bear,
You are most difficult to scare."

And now this rather curious three,
Sit down together and have tea.

The hermit says, "You must not stay,
My dog will take you on your way."

They leave by yet another door,
That Rupert has not seen before.

"Oho, so a little bird has been telling you my secrets, has he?" laughs the old man. "Well, well it's quite true. I don't want visitors and I could have pulled a lever and shut that iron door before you got in, but I have watched you on the hillside and I liked the way you stood up to my dog when he rushed at you and pretended to be fierce, so I allowed you to come in in spite of your inquisitiveness. Now let's have tea and you shall tell me your name."

Rupert is delighted at the way things have turned out and he tells the old gentleman his name and all about himself. "It's a topping cave you have here," he says. "And I wish I knew how you trained this wonderful dog. May I bring my pal to see you?" "No, you certainly may not," smiles the old man. "You've disturbed me enough already. So now good-bye." The dog rises at once to lead Rupert away through yet another rocky tunnel.

RUPERT TELLS HIS STORY

"Where am I now?" asks Rupert – but
At once the heavy door is shut.

Just then Bill Badger comes in sight,
Relieved to find his chum all right.

A farmhand kindly came along,
To help in case things had gone wrong.

But all has ended happily,
As Bill and Rupert both agree.

When he reaches the open-air Rupert gazes around. "Please how do I get back to where I entered?" he asks. But the only answer is a loud clang. Another iron door has dropped suddenly, and the dog has disappeared. Rather anxiously he climbs to a higher point and down below him he spies his pal Bill Badger. "Oh, Rupert, are you safe?" cries Bill, breathlessly. "I couldn't find a policeman, but this farm worker heard what happened and has come to help you. Do tell how you got out."

The farmhand doesn't wait to be told. "You've bin meetin' our silent dawg, I'll be bound," he laughs. "And I'll lay he's led you a pretty dance. But I see he's done you no harm. He never does. So I'll leave you and get back to my work." He says good-bye Dod Rupert takes the arm of his pal. "It's high time we went home," he smiles. "We do meet some odd people on our walks and the old hermit certainly was funny. Come on and I'll tell you all about it."

AN EASY WAY TO MAKE

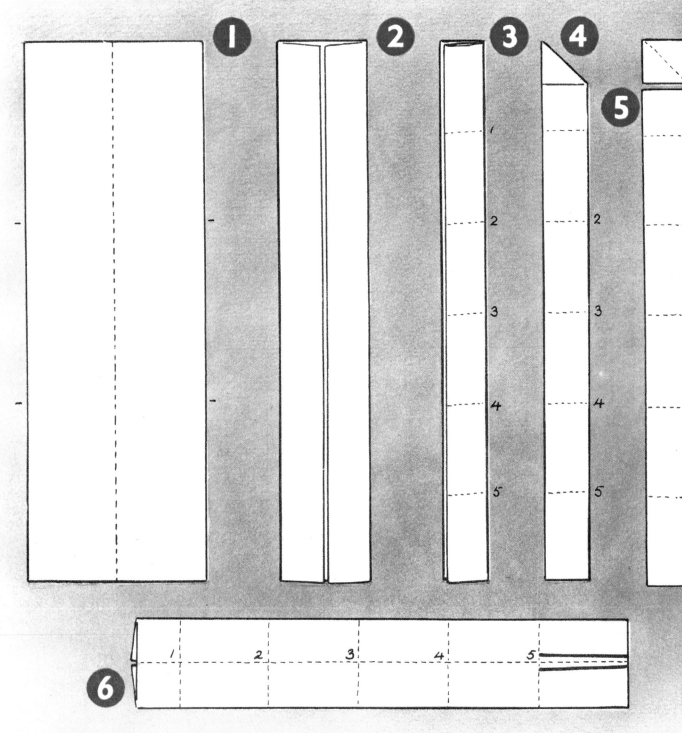

Your dog will look even jollier with a tiny bow of ribbon tied round his neck.

To make this Scottie dog you need a piece of thin, strong paper three times as long as it is broad. Fold it in half to give the dotted line in Fig. 1. Turn the sides to the middle line (Fig. 2), press flat and fold in half lengthwise (Fig. 3). Mark into six equal parts and number the dividing lines 1 to 5.

Fold down the top corner (Fig. 4), cut off the square you have made (Fig. 5) and throw it away. Next partly open the paper (as in Fig 2) and make two cuts from the edge through the last section as shown in Fig. 6. Be careful to cut only one thickness of paper. This will be the dog's tail so make it narrower at the end.

Then refold the last two sections but reverse the middle fold for sections

RUPERT'S PAPER SCOTTIE

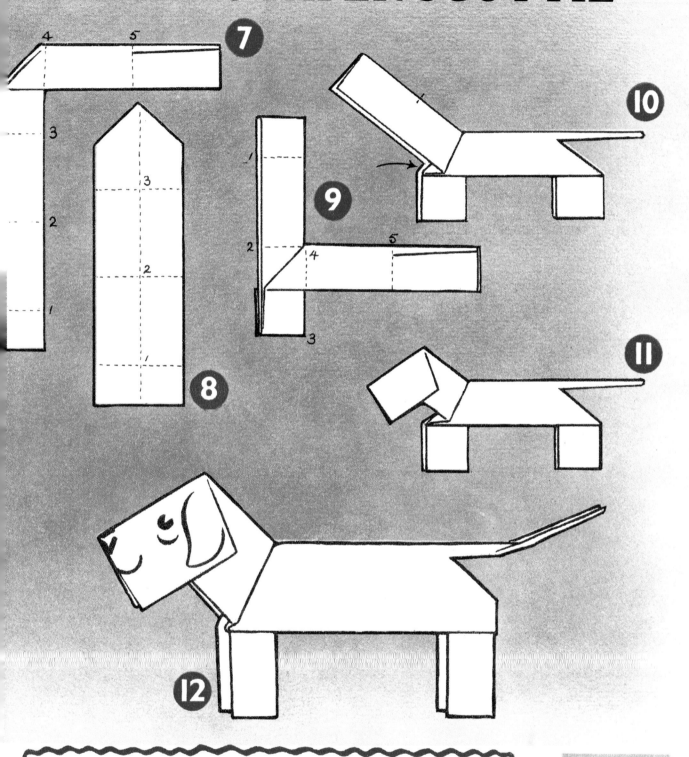

one to four and turn down at right angles to give Fig. 7. Open out sections one to four (Fig. 8), turn up the lower part along division three and close the sides as in Fig. 9.

Now bend the upper part forward, opening slightly so that the resulting folds (arrowed) can be pressed flat (Fig. 10). Also fold the section below the tail inward and downward for the hind legs. Next mark a point rather less than halfway up the sloping edge and bend the top portion forward again, pressing the folds as before (Fig. 11).

Cut the front legs apart. If all the legs look too thick fold part of each one inwards (Fig. 12). Press all folds very firmly. Lastly draw the dog's face.

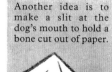

Another idea is to make a slit at the dog's mouth to hold a bone cut out of paper.

RUPERT'S
Country Puzzle

Rupert has an afternoon's holiday from school, so he sets out for his favourite spot in the country, hoping to meet some of his little friends of the fields and woods. It is his lucky day, for he finds some of them gathered on a sandy slope. "Why, there's the rabbit and the robin and the hedgehog," he whispers, edging his way up a grassy bank, "and there's the squirrel too!"

He looks further and sees a mole and a harvest mouse. "Fancy finding six all at once!" he thinks. "If I keep very still, I can watch them from here." Each circle shows the home of one of the creatures. Can you tell which is which? Some are easy, but others may make you think hard. Write your list, then check the answers at the bottom of this page and see how many you have got right.

Answers: 1 - Robin, 2 - Harvest Mouse, 3 - Mole, 4 - Squirrel, 5 - Rabbit, 6 - Hedgehog

RUPERT and

*One morning, Rupert wakes to find
Ice patterns Jack Frost's left behind . . .*

One winter morning, Rupert wakes up to find icy patterns all over his bedroom window . . . "Jack Frost must have been here!" he laughs. "He draws on everyone's windows when winter starts!" The patterns are so pretty that Rupert calls for his mother to come and see. "How lovely!" she smiles. "The sun makes them sparkle like diamonds!" Rupert wonders if Jack is still in Nutwood. "Perhaps he'd let *me* draw patterns?"

the Deep Freeze

"How beautiful!" smiles Mrs Bear.
"They must mean Winter's in the air!"

"I'll look for Jack! Perhaps he'll know
When Nutwood's due to have some snow . . ."

As soon as he has finished breakfast, Rupert puts on his scarf and hurries outside. It is a crisp, sunny morning but very cold . . . "We must be due for snow soon!" he thinks. "I wonder if Jack knows when?" There is no sign of anyone in the village, so Rupert decides to look for his friend on Nutwood Common. Jack Frost normally stays out of sight as he goes about his business, but Rupert finally spots him, standing all alone . . .

"There's Jack Frost now! But what's he found?
It looks like something on the ground . . ."

RUPERT MEETS JACK FROST

Then Rupert realises he
Has lost something. "What can it be?"

"My ice thermometer!" says Jack.
"For freezing things! I need it back!"

"I'll help you search," says Rupert. "For
It must be somewhere here – I'm sure!"

No matter how hard Rupert tries
He finds no sign. "It's gone!" he sighs.

To Rupert's surprise, Jack Frost seems to be searching for something. "Hello!" he calls and hurries to join him. "Who's there?" says Jack. "Oh, Rupert! I was so busy I didn't hear you coming . . ." "What have you lost?" asks Rupert. "My thermometer," sighs Jack. "I'll be in trouble unless I find it!" "We've got one," says Rupert. "Not like mine," says Jack. "It freezes everything it touches. I use it to draw on window panes. My father gave it to me as a special present!"

Rupert offers to help search for the missing thermometer. "It looks like an icicle," Jack tells him. "Be careful not to touch the tip, or else it will freeze you too!" The pair split up, with Rupert combing the common while Jack covers the rest of Nutwood . . . "I can't see an icicle!" thinks Rupert. "Perhaps it's fallen into one of these bushes or got buried in a clump of grass?" The longer Rupert searches, the harder it seems. "Like looking for a needle in a haystack!" he sighs.

RUPERT FINDS A FROZEN POND

Then someone calls out Rupert's name.
"Hey! Come and join our sliding game!"

"A frozen pond!" he blinks. "What fun!
It's big enough for everyone . . ."

The pals walk home and Rupert sees
The fountain's not begun to freeze . . .

His parents think it's strange the way
That only one pond froze today . . .

Rupert is still looking for Jack Frost's thermometer when he hears the sound of laughter. "It's Podgy and the others!" he smiles. "They're sliding on a frozen pond!" Hurrying to join his chums, he hears how the Fox brothers found the pond and couldn't resist trying it out. "Why don't you have a go?" calls Freddy. "The ice is so thick, it's quite safe!" Rupert takes a run up, then goes whizzing after the others. "Hurrah!" he cries as they slither and slide, over and over again.

At last, the chums have had enough of their game and everyone makes their way back to Nutwood. "It's odd that nothing else is frozen!" thinks Rupert. "The village fountain normally stops as soon as the weather turns icy but it's flowing as fast as ever . . ." Rupert's parents are surprised to hear about the frozen pond as well. "How odd!" says Mrs Bear. "Perhaps a freak wind chilled the pond!" "That must be it!" nods Rupert's father. "The barometer said we'd have sunshine . . ."

RUPERT IS MYSTIFIED

Next morning, Mr Bear finds more
Ice patterns – different from before . . .

"A funny drawing!" Rupert blinks.
"That can't be Jack Frost's work!" he thinks.

His mother gives a startled cry.
"My washing's like a board!" But why?

"It must have frozen in the night."
"My word!" gasps Mr Bear, "you're right!"

Next morning, Rupert comes downstairs to find a new set of icy patterns on the window panes. "They look different today!" says Mr Bear. "The ones in the kitchen were more like scribble than pretty flowers . . ." Peering outside, he gives a gasp of surprise, then calls Rupert over to see. "I don't believe it!" he tuts, "it must be one of your chums!" Rupert peers at the drawing. "That doesn't look like one of Jack Frost's drawings!" he says. "But who else could have made it?"

When breakfast is over, Rupert and his parents find more surprises out in the garden . . . "Come and look at my washing!" cries Mrs Bear. "It's frozen stiff!" "Impossible!" says Rupert's father. "The lawn isn't even white . . ." Unpegging a shirt from the line, he holds it up, then shakes his head in disbelief. "Are you sure you didn't use too much starch?" he blinks. "No!" says Mrs Bear. "It's all cold and icy. We must have had a sudden frost overnight."

RUPERT SLIPS ON THE ICE

The High Street's frozen too, it seems
The icy pavement glints and gleams . . .

"Help!" Rupert cries. He stops his fall
By clutching at a nearby wall!

A lorry's slipped as well. Its load
Is scattered all across the road!

Then Rupert stops, amazed at how
The village fountain's frozen now . . .

Leaving his parents to puzzle over the frozen washing, Rupert sets off towards the High Street in search of his chums. He hasn't gone far, when he sees a crowd of people gathered together by the side of the road. Hurrying towards them, he finds the pavement is covered in a fine layer of slippery ice. "There must have been a frost after all!" he gasps. "I wonder why it seems so patchy?" Clutching the top of the wall, he sets off again to see why everyone is staring.

When Rupert reaches the High Street, the crowd is so large that he has to push forward to see what is causing the commotion. A lorry has skidded on a patch of ice and shed its load! Parcels and packages lie in a jumbled heap as P.C. Growler tries to clear the way. "It's lucky no-one was hurt!" says Mrs Badger. "Yes!" nods the Professor. "I'm amazed everywhere's so icy!" Just look at the village fountain . . ." To Rupert's astonishment, it is completely covered in ice!

RUPERT SOLVES THE MYSTERY

The Fox twins shuffle past the throng.
A bandaged Ferdy limps along . . .

"The fountain froze so fast he fell
And dropped the magic wand as well!"

"Wand?" Rupert asks. The twins admit
They drew on window panes with it . . .

There, in the fountain, Rupert sees
Jack's missing wand that makes things freeze!

Rupert is still marvelling at the fountain when he spots the Fox brothers coming out of Dr Lion's surgery. Poor Ferdy has his foot bandaged up and is hobbling along with a stick. "What's happened?" asks Rupert. "Did you slip on the ice?" "That's right," says Freddy. "It froze so quickly we were taken by surprise." "Goodness!" blinks Rupert. "I've never heard of ice freezing *that* fast before. Where did you fall?" "From the fountain!" says Ferdy. "I slid off and dropped the magic wand!"

"Magic wand?" asks Rupert. "Yes," says Ferdy. "We found it up on the common. . ." "Jack Frost's thermometer!" Rupert cries. "He uses it to draw patterns on everyone's windows." "*We* tried that!" admits Freddy. "Then we found we could freeze things as well!" Leading Rupert to the fountain's edge, he points down at a glowing light. "*That's* what's making everything icy!" he explains. "The water froze so quickly we couldn't get it back. Now the ice is spreading, all over Nutwood!"

RUPERT TELLS THE PROFESSOR

"Hello!" the old Professor cries.
"This ice is rather a surprise!"

Rupert explains he knows what's made
The ice. "It's trapped here, I'm afraid!"

The professor tells Bodkin they
Will need a blow-lamp straightaway . . .

"We need to melt the ice before
This magic wand makes any more!"

As Rupert and Freddy peer down into the ice, they are joined by the Professor, who has come to take a closer look at the fountain. "Fascinating!" he declares. "Everything seems to have frozen so fast!" "Perhaps!" gulps Freddy. "Can't think why! I'd better be off now, Rupert. Got to help Ferdy get home . . ." Without mentioning the Foxes, Rupert tells the Professor how Jack Frost's thermometer is frozen inside the fountain. "That's why Nutwood has suddenly grown so cold!"

While most people would be astonished by Rupert's story, the Professor simply nods his head. "Of course! If the thermometer makes things cold, then ice will go on forming until it's taken out of the fountain . . ." He thinks for a moment, then sends Bodkin to his workshop to fetch a blow-lamp. "Thawing the ice is our only hope," he explains as his servant comes hurrying back. "Chipping it away would take far too long. If something's not done soon, the whole village will be iced-up . . ."

RUPERT IS DISAPPOINTED

The blow-lamp starts to thaw the ice.
"We'll have the wand free in a trice!"

To everyone's dismay they see
The ice re-forming instantly!

Next morning ice is everywhere.
"It's freezing cold!" says Mrs Bear.

The fountain's disappeared from sight
Beneath an icy mound of white . . .

Bodkin points the blow-lamp at the frozen fountain. "It's melting!" smiles Rupert. "The moment he's finished, I'll reach in and grab Jack's thermometer . . ." Soon Bodkin pushes back his goggles and turns off the lamp. "That's better," he declares, but, to Rupert's dismay, the water freezes over. "Try again!" orders the Professor, but it's no use. Each time the ice melts, it freezes straightaway. "What a dilemma!" he sighs. "We'll have to think of something else . . ."

Next morning, the ice from the fountain has spread so far it covers the whole village . . . "You'll need to wrap up warm!" says Mrs Bear as she hands Rupert his coat. "Be careful not to slip, dear. The path looks like a skating rink!" As he sets off along the High Street, there are icicles hanging from every window and the fountain has vanished under a frozen mound. "The Professor's here already!" he smiles as he spots his old friend, standing by the fountain, lost in thought . . .

RUPERT FLIES NORTH

The old Professor can't think how
To stop the ice from spreading now . . .

At last the friends agree to go
And wait for Jack Frost. "He might know!"

"We're flying North, across the sea.
Rupert can navigate for me . . ."

The pair take off and quickly find
They've left the English coast behind . . .

The Professor stares at the fountain and shakes his head. "It's no use!" he declares. "Each time we melt the ice it's sure to freeze again . . ." "Jack Frost's thermometer's causing the trouble!" says Rupert. "If we told *him* what's happened, he might know how to stop it!" "Good idea!" nods the Professor. "He lives at the North Pole, doesn't he?" "That's right," says Rupert. "His father has a palace made of ice." "Come on!" says the Professor. "We'll fly there, straightaway . . ."

As soon as the pair reach the Professor's tower, he leads the way to his latest aircraft. "There's only room for two of us," he tells Bodkin. "You stay here, while Rupert helps me navigate." The little servant fills the plane's fuel tank and helps Rupert clamber into the cockpit. The Professor starts the engine and soon they are soaring high over Nutwood, off towards the coast. "I'll keep flying North towards the Pole!" calls the Professor. "Tell me when you spot the palace . . ."

RUPERT ENCOUNTERS A SNOWSTORM

Icebergs and jagged peaks appear.
"The North Pole must be getting near . . ."

A sudden snowstorm starts to blow –
The pair can't see which way to go!

"Who knows how long this storm might last?
We'll have to land until it's passed . . ."

"We'll wait until the snow stops then
I'll try to find the Pole again!"

For a long time, all that Rupert can see is the blue of the ocean down below. At last, he spots the jagged peaks of distant mountains and massive icebergs. "This is the start of the Polar ice!" says the Professor. "We shouldn't have much further to go . . ." As he speaks, a dark cloud looms on the horizon, growing larger and larger, until it fills the whole sky. "A snowstorm!" gasps Rupert, as icy winds buffet the little plane. "We'll have to land!" calls the Professor. "I can't see where I'm going!"

By the time the little plane lands it is completely covered in a thick layer of snow. "This is terrible!" groans the Professor. "The blizzard has blown us off course and I can't tell where we are . . ." Unfolding a map, he shows Rupert the path they were taking and the spot where the Pole should be. "We'll just have to wait till it stops snowing!" he declares. "If we leave the plane now we're bound to get lost. When the blizzard's over I'll use my compass to find the way."

RUPERT MEETS UNCLE POLAR

Then, suddenly a polar bear
Surprises the astonished pair!

It's Rupert's Uncle Polar, who
Lives nearby, in a large igloo . . .

"Come in!" he smiles delightedly.
"You've just dropped by in time for tea!"

Polar agrees to guide the friends.
"We'll set off when this blizzard ends . . ."

Suddenly, Rupert hears someone tapping at the window of the plane. "A wild polar bear!" gasps the Professor. "Uncle Polar!" cries Rupert. *"He's* not wild. He lives at the North Pole . . ." Rupert's uncle is delighted to see the visitors from Nutwood and invites them to come and shelter in his igloo. "The snowstorm should blow over in a while," he says. "Come and tell me what you're up to!" The Professor blinks in surprise as Polar leads the way across the snow to his special house . . .

The Professor is even more surprised to see *inside* the igloo, for Polar's house is far bigger than it seems . . . "Come and have tea!" he says. "It's nice to have guests drop in. I don't get many visitors." When he hears how Nutwood has been covered in ice, Polar agrees that King Frost is the only person who can sort things out. "He lives in a great ice palace, quite near the Pole. I'll take you there when this blizzard stops. It's easy to find when you know the way . . ."

RUPERT SETS OUT

"Clear skies!" smiles Polar. "Time to go!
I'll lead the way across the snow!"

The Professor says he'll fly back
While Rupert goes to visit Jack.

"Jack's father's palace lies nearby
The Northern Lights. Just watch the sky . . ."

"It's like a rainbow!" Rupert blinks.
"And that must be Jack's home!" he thinks.

When everyone has finished tea, Uncle Polar steps outside to see if the blizzard is over. "Clear skies!" he calls. "We won't be troubled again . . ." As Polar knows King Frost, he offers to take Rupert to the ice palace while the Professor flies back to Nutwood. "Good idea!" smiles the Professor. "I'll tell your parents you're in safe hands. If you need any help, just give me a call!" Climbing back into the plane, he starts the engine and is soon soaring off, up into the sky.

Uncle Polar sets off towards King Frost's palace. "You'll know we're getting near when you spot the Northern Lights!" he says. "Keep watching until you see the sky change colour . . ." Rupert follows his uncle across the snowy wastes, amazed that he can find the way. "It's my home!" laughs Polar. "In Nutwood, *you'd* have to show *me* where to go!" After a while, the sky turns from blue to pink, then to a brilliant green. "Northern Lights!" smiles Polar. "And there's King Frost's palace . . ."

RUPERT ENTERS THE ICE PALACE

The pair approach a palace where
Two guards stand sentry. "Halt! Who's there?"

When Polar mentions King Frost's son
They say he can't see anyone. . .

"I'm sure King Frost will talk to me!
I'd like to see him urgently!"

At last the guard agrees to bring
The pair to see Jack and the King. . .

As they approach the glittering palace, Rupert sees two sentries guarding the main gate. "Who's there?" they ask. "What business have you with King Frost?" "I've come to see his son," replies Rupert. "Jack and I have often met, during his winter visits to Nutwood . . ." "Young Master Jack is in disgrace for losing his thermometer!" declares the guard. "The King has forbidden him any visitors for the rest of the week. If you want to see him, you'll have to come back later . . ."

"Impossible!" cries Uncle Polar. "Rupert has come here on an urgent mission! Tell King Frost I *insist* on seeing him." The guard delivers Polar's message and soon comes back to announce that the King will receive them immediately. As he enters the throne room Rupert spots Jack, still being scolded by his father. "Oh, dear!" he thinks. "I hope he won't be too cross when he hears what's happened. Supposing he decides it serves us right and leaves Nutwood to freeze all winter?"

RUPERT ASKS KING FROST TO HELP

The King hears how the wand Jack dropped
Will freeze Nutwood unless it's stopped.

"Fetch thawing powder straightaway –
We need to act without delay!"

In no time, Jack comes running back
And hands the King a little sack.

"Watch!" says King Frost. "This powder's sure
To make the thickest ice all thaw!"

Although King Frost looks cross, he nods to Uncle Polar and asks what brings his nephew all the way to the North Pole. When he hears how the lost thermometer has covered Nutwood in a layer of ice, he shakes his head and declares it is all a result of Jack's carelessness. "*You* caused the Freeze, so *you* shall help to end it!" he tell his son. "Fetch a sack of thawing powder from the cellar as quickly as you can. Tell the guards to make sure it's the strongest they can find . . ."

To Rupert's surprise, Jack returns with a small sack, hardly bigger than a bag of flour . . . "Well done!" says the King. "This should solve Nutwood's problems, but I'll test a little first, to make sure it works . . ." Taking a pinch of powder from the sack, he sprinkles it on the frozen window-sill. Almost at once, the ice begins to melt, vanishing before Rupert's astonished gaze. "Double strength!" says the King. "Thaws ice and snow in a blink of an eye!"

RUPERT LEAVES THE PALACE

Rupert and Polar thank the King.
His powder should solve everything . . .

They say goodbye to Jack Frost too.
"I'll send the wand straight back to you!"

Then Rupert asks his uncle how
He'll travel back to Nutwood now.

"Don't worry!" Polar smiles. "You'll see!
There's something you can take for me . . ."

"I *knew* you would be able to help!" says Polar as he takes the thawing powder from King Frost. "We polar bears enjoy ice and snow all year round, but down in Nutwood they don't like being too chilly!" Rupert tells Jack that he'll get his thermometer back for him as soon as the fountain melts. "I'm sure your father won't be cross for long! You didn't *mean* to freeze Nutwood. It was only an accident, after all!" "Come on!" says Uncle Polar. "It's time we were on our way . . ."

"How am I going to get to Nutwood?" asks Rupert as the pair walk back across the snow. "Will you telephone the Professor and ask him to collect me?" "Don't worry!" laughs Polar. "There's someone else who can take you even faster than the Professor's plane. We've arranged to meet at my igloo, just after tea-time . . ." As they near Polar's house, Rupert can see no sign of a visitor. "Who is it?" he asks "You'll see!" smiles his uncle.

RUPERT MEETS SANTA

Rupert tells Polar he can hear
The sound of sleigh bells drawing near . . .

"It's Santa Claus! He's in his sleigh –
Piled high with toys for Christmas day!"

"Hello!" blinks Santa. "Rupert Bear
From Nutwood! I'm just going there!"

"You'd better fly back home with me!"
The pair take off immediately . . .

The moment they arrive at the igloo, Uncle Polar unlocks a cupboard and reaches inside. "There's a special package I want you to take . . ." he begins, but breaks off as Rupert hears the sound of jingling bells. "Look outside!" chuckles Polar. When Rupert crawls out of the igloo he is astonished to see a reindeer-drawn sledge swooping down from the sky. "Santa Claus!" he gasps. "Of course! It's Christmas Eve. He must be on his way to deliver all the children's presents."

Santa is astonished to see Rupert at the North Pole. "I thought you'd be in Nutwood!" he says. "I'm just on my way there to deliver all your presents." "That's why Santa's come visiting!" laughs Polar. "He was going to take a present from me as well . . ." When he hears how Rupert plans to save Nutwood from being buried in ice, Santa agrees to take him there on his sledge. "You're lucky it's the next place on my list," he says. "I hope we won't find it's too icy to land . . ."

RUPERT RETURNS TO NUTWOOD

The sky grows dark and stars come out.
"There won't be anyone about . . ."

They spot the village, down below,
"It looks as if it's thick with snow!"

"The fountain!" Rupert calls. "I'll try
To sprinkle dust as we fly by . . ."

The ice all disappears and then
The fountain starts to work again!

Darkness falls as Santa's reindeer speed on their way to Nutwood. Rupert explains how King Frost has given him a sack full of special powder to thaw the frozen village. "There it is now!" he calls excitedly. "I can see the church tower and everybody's houses . . ." "They should all be tucked up in bed by now," says Santa. "We'll fly over the rooftops and you can sprinkle your powder without being seen. It looks so white and frosty, you'd almost think it had been snowing!"

Santa's sleigh circles over the sleeping village, flying lower and lower, until Rupert spots Nutwood's frozen fountain. Carefully untying King Frost's sack of powder, he reaches over the side and sprinkles a generous handful on the huge mound of ice . . . "I'll land nearby, so we can see if there's any change," announces Santa. By the time the sleigh stops, Rupert is sure he can hear the sound of splashing. "Look!" he gasps. "It's working! The fountain has thawed already . . ."

RUPERT RECOVERS JACK'S WAND

*"I've got it!" Rupert cries. "Now Jack
Can have his thermometer back!"*

*"Well done! Give me the powder too.
I'll sprinkle all the rest for you!"*

*Next morning, Rupert wakes to find
A present Santa's left behind . . .*

*"Skates!" Rupert laughs. "Although they're nice
I think we've had enough of ice!"*

Peering into the trough of the fountain, Rupert can see Jack Frost's thermometer, glowing at the bottom. Rolling up his sleeve, he reaches down and lifts it to the surface. "At last!" he cries. "To think it's caused all this trouble . . ." Santa tells Rupert that he will take the thermometer back to Jack when he returns to the North Pole. "I'll take the rest of your powder too," he adds. "I can sprinkle it over Nutwood as I put everyone's presents down the chimney pots."

Next morning, Rupert wakes to find the ice has already melted. At the foot of his bed is a colourful stocking full of presents. "There's the parcel Uncle Polar gave me!" he thinks and hurries to unwrap it straightaway. "Ice skates!" laugh his parents when they see what he has been given. "Normally, I'd wish for a snowy Christmas!" smiles Rupert, "But after all that's happened, I don't mind waiting a little while before I try them out . . ."

THE END

114

Your Own Rupert Story

Title: _____

Why not try colouring the pictures below and writing a story to fit them? Write your story in four parts, one for each picture, saying what it shows. Then, faintly in pencil, print each part neatly on the lines under its picture. When they fit, go over the printing with a ball-pen. There is space at the top for a title.

RUPERT'S MEMORY GAME

After you have read all the stories in this book, you can play Rupert's fun Memory Game! Study the pictures below. Each is part of a bigger picture you will have seen in the stories. Can you answer the questions at the bottom of the page? Afterwards, check the stories to discover if you were right.

NOW TRY TO REMEMBER . . .

1. Who does this little cat belong to?
2. Who finds Dr Lion?
3. What is happening here?
4. What is the imp saying to Rupert?
5. Who is this?
6. Who is Rupert helping?
7. What are the Guides pointing to?
8. Why is Rupert in the tree?
9. What game is Rupert playing?
10. Where is this?
11. Where does this railcar lead?
12. What is happening in this picture?
13. Who is the dog's owner?
14. Who made this drawing?
15. Why is the Professor surprised?
16. Who is Rupert about to meet?

Follow
RUPERT
in the
DAILY EXPRESS
every morning

Published by the London Express Newspaper Ltd., and Printed by L.T.A. Robinson Ltd., London, S.W.9